the
protectors
PETE JOHNSON

mammoth

First published in Great Britain 1998
by Mammoth, an imprint of Egmont Children's Books Limited
Michelin House, 81 Fulham Road, London SW3 6RB

Text copyright © 1998 Pete Johnson

Cover illustration copyright © 1998 David Kearney

The moral rights of the author and cover illustration have been asserted.

ISBN 0 7497 3256 3

10 9 8 7 6 5 4 3 2

A CIP catalogue record for this title is available from the British Library

Typeset by Avon Dataset Ltd, Bidford on Avon, Warwickshire
Printed in Great Britain by Cox & Wyman Ltd, Reading, Berkshire

'I wonder what it is that makes us care for one another.'

George Eliot

One

Greg was being watched again.

The same guy as before, wearing the same long black jumper, was standing by the school door. It was as if he were waiting for him. Greg gazed across the playground. He sensed danger.

'Don't make eye contact,' his dad had told him when a man had started yelling at everyone on the railway platform. Maybe Dad's advice would work now. Greg reached into his briefcase for the book he'd just put away: it was one of his favourites, *The Hound of the Baskervilles*. Greg had brought the book along two weeks ago, when he'd started at this school. It was like being accompanied by an old friend. He'd just got to one of the best bits where Sherlock Holmes and Dr Watson were on the moors. Greg started to read.

The boy was walking towards him. Greg raised the book even higher, his heart thumping. If only he could jump inside this story; hide there until the boy had gone past. He peered at the book so intently the words began to swim.

Suddenly the boy eased Greg's case out of his grasp almost before he realised anything.

Greg stared up at him. 'What are you doing?'

The boy ignored him. He was examining the case. He ran his fingers all over it, then he held it up and shook it. 'What's in here?'

'Oh, just my pens and pencils and my school books. Why do you want to know?'

The boy didn't reply. He was too busy smelling the case. He ran his nose right along the top of it, then sniffed as if he were a connoisseur. It smelled of leather. That was the only thing Greg liked about it.

He hadn't wanted a briefcase at all. He'd asked for a sports bag – preferably blue or dark red – and he'd listed some good brand names. But his parents wanted to surprise him; they'd saved up to buy him the best. Their faces broke into smiles when they saw how smart Greg looked. How could he tell them this briefcase had absolutely no street cred? How could he tell them about all the jokes and comments this briefcase would cause? He couldn't.

The boy looked at Greg. 'Bit flash, isn't it?'

'I know, I hate it, but my parents got it for me, so what can you do?' Greg shrugged his shoulders and smiled hopefully at the boy. The boy didn't smile back.

'I do know how terrible it is.' He was pleading now, pleading forgiveness for his parents' bad taste, yet he had a tiny flare of hope as well; the case which had marked him out looked nerdish, not him.

Greg plucked up courage. 'May I have it back now, please?'

A faint gleam came into the boy's eyes. He was two or three years older than Greg but he wasn't particularly big. He had very long arms which made him look gangly. He was slightly stooped with short, reddy-brown hair, pasty skin and major freckles. His eyes were pale and oddly blank. His black jumper was full of holes. 'Will you let me carry your bag for you?' he asked politely.

Greg wasn't sure how to react. All week older boys had barged past him, just laughing when he'd got lost and asked for directions. But now, suddenly, one of them was offering to carry his bag.

The boy smiled at Greg, but he only smiled with half of his face. Greg became more and more uneasy, yet he didn't dare to refuse. The boy was walking alongside him as if they were the best of mates. 'What's your name?' he asked.

'Greg. What's yours?'

'Neil.' His voice was low and husky. 'You look a real office boy with this.' He gave another half-smile.

Greg laughed nervously. Then, just for something to say, 'What's your bag like, then?'

'I haven't got a bag . . . don't need one. Never have.'

Greg wasn't sure how to answer so they walked along in silence. The corridors were teeming with boys, but Neil didn't have to push through. Everyone just moved out of his way.

To Greg's relief his form room was just ahead. 'I'm in there,' he said pointing.

'I know,' Neil replied and strolled right into the form room and placed the briefcase on Greg's desk, as if he were a porter.

'Thank you very much,' gasped Greg.

'Don't mention it.' Then he gave a kind of bow and murmured, 'I'll be in contact.'

*

Josh was outraged.

They hadn't even given him a table. They'd just thrown four chairs into a semicircle. He couldn't work like that. He wouldn't. He and Andy had to 'borrow' a table (Josh's school didn't have any desks) from another classroom. It took up half the room and it still wasn't right.

'This table is nowhere near high enough,' announced Josh. 'I want to really glare down at the sad specimens who come to see us . . . and their chair shouldn't be the same as ours. They should have one of those wooden chairs with a dodgy back, or a stool.'

'Or why not just get them to sit on the floor?' joked Andy. 'After they've licked your boots, of course.'

Josh had placed himself behind the table. He sat right in the centre. Andy hovered on the edge. He arched his eyebrows and sniffed. 'This room stinks.'

'Well, it hasn't been used since the Middle Ages,' said Josh. 'It used to be the school nurse's room.' He looked round at a sink, some shelves, a radiator, a cupboard and on top of the cupboard, a fridge that could fit snugly into a dolls' house. 'Still, it's got possibilities.'

'But do you think anyone's going to turn up?' asked Andy.

'That's a very good question.'

'I'm glad you liked it.'

'Yes, someone will come,' said Josh, suddenly very confident. He smacked his lips. 'I'm looking forward to that. And don't forget, we can summon people here.'

Last week Josh and Andy had discovered a new way to skive lessons: training as anti-bullying counsellors. They'd duly signed up for this extra little holiday. They'd sat giggling and playing hangman during the talks and games, although they had quite enjoyed the role-playing: they'd acted the parts of a boy who no one liked because he had smelly trainers and of his tormentor.

This was their first day on duty and now any younger pupil who had a problem with bullying could come to them for help.

'Still, what do we care if no one turns up?' said Josh. 'I reckon we can spin this out for months. So, in the winter when everyone else is outside freezing to death, we'll be tucked away in here.'

Actually Josh was eager for at least one caller. And a few moments later there was a polite knock on the door.

'We're in business,' said Josh. 'Enter.'

'Enter?' repeated Andy scornfully. 'You're not the headmaster.'

Mr Denton, the teacher in charge of the anti-bullying scheme, put his head round the door.

'Ah, Mr Denton, have you come for a consultation?' said Josh at once. Mr Denton was in fact experiencing some classroom discipline problems himself. He'd only joined the school last term, one of a posse of new teachers appointed when half of the older teachers had taken early retirement – in some cases very early retirement. So suddenly the school was full of these bright new faces. The pupils had rubbed their hands gleefully, anticipating some fun.

In Mr Denton's first lesson he'd handed round a plan of a classroom and asked the pupils to fill in their names. Josh had called himself Elvis Brown so for the next two lessons Mr Denton addressed him by that name. He never quite recovered control of the class after that.

Josh regretted it now. He rather liked Mr Denton, especially after Josh had completely misunderstood an essay title and Mr Denton had taken him aside and spent some time explaining the real meaning to him. He would have been a good teacher if only he hadn't stood so awkwardly and had this slightly apologetic air whenever he told anyone off. He was also very young-looking even though most of his hair had already migrated, earning him his nickname, Desert Head.

Mr Denton sat down and smiled keenly. He was keen about most things. 'So, how's it all going, then?'

'Very well,' said Josh. 'We've had enquiries already and I'm sure the word will soon get round – about my amazing abilities.'

'I'm sure it will,' said Mr Denton with a smile. He sat back in his chair. He thought Josh was a bit of a card. He had even laughed when he discovered Josh wasn't really called Elvis Brown. 'Now, do you need anything at all, boys?'

'A coffee machine would be nice,' said Josh.

'In here?'

Josh nodded solemnly. 'The smell of coffee relaxes people, don't you think, so they'll be more ready to tell Andy and me their problems?'

'I really don't think we could manage a coffee machine, but maybe I could get you a kettle and . . .'

'Ah, but then,' said Josh, 'if I have to go off and make them coffee, it could break the atmosphere. Still, Andy makes a mean cup of coffee, so I suppose he could do that.'

'Listen to him,' said Andy.

'And we'll need biscuits too,' went on Josh. 'Milk chocolate, not plain. I don't like plain, do you? And we don't want crunchy biscuits, because people might have to spit the bits out when they're talking and that could stop them sharing their problems, couldn't it?'

'I really want this to work,' said Mr Denton, 'because I'm worried about some of the boys here, especially the younger ones. Sometimes I see them and they look scared out of their wits . . . they won't tell me anything. But something is going on here. Something bad.'

Josh tried hard to look grave and concerned. But honestly, what was Desert Head raving on about? Of course younger boys got picked on, of course there was bullying and fights. There always had been and always would be. It was part of life, like your voice breaking, and waking up one morning with a face full of zits.

Josh remembered how as a first year he had been goaded into a fight with an older boy at the top of the playing field. Word quickly spread. A massive circle of boys loomed round them. Josh got the worst of it and tried to leave, but the older boys pushed him back. He had to carry on. It was one of the worst moments of his life. He ended up well and truly defeated but he'd shown he could fight back and no one ever picked a fight with him again.

Mr Denton got up. 'Well, I'd better go just in case someone is trying to see you. Don't want a teacher cluttering up the place. Oh, if you could keep the noise down. The caretaker's office is next door and I don't think he's too keen on this project.'

'What a surprise,' murmured Andy.

It was the caretaker, more than any of the teachers, who demanded to know what pupils were doing hanging round in reception, who told them to stop running in the corridor and chased them off his flower beds, or his 'garden' as he called it, at the front of the school.

'We'll tell all our clients to whisper,' said Josh.

Mr Denton paused for a moment. 'You know, I think younger boys might come and chat to you two.'

'I'm sure they will,' said Josh in a voice oozing sincerity. 'Don't worry, Sir, we'll make a real success of this . . . and don't forget about the coffee and biscuits, will you?'

There was a definite spring in Greg's step. At football this afternoon he had surprised a few people with his skill. He was really quite a decent player and his rating had definitely gone up. Not that he'd been unpopular before, despite being quiet.

There was another boy in his form who was always picked on: a small, ginger-haired boy called Eric. Greg thought Eric brought it on himself: if someone even touched him he started squealing, so of course, everyone wanted to hear Eric squeal. It became a kind of game.

Greg reached the school gates. He dug into his bag for *The Hound of the Baskervilles* and stopped suddenly. His breath caught in his throat. By the school gates were four boys, all on mopeds. Standing in the middle of them was Neil. Earlier a boy from another class had warned Greg, 'I saw you chatting with Neil. You don't want to get too friendly with him, you know. One day he'll be sharing his sweets that he's just nicked with you, the next he'll be slamming your head in the locker. Or he'll get someone else to do it.' Before Greg could ask him any questions the boy had gone. More than anything Greg wanted to stay out of Neil's way but what could he do when Neil was standing right in front of him?

Greg threaded his way through the throng of mopeds, no one moved. Then, out of politeness, he said hello to Neil, very quietly, very respectfully.

Neil looked straight at him. His face was cool, expressionless and then he heard Neil call his name. 'Gregory.'

Greg turned round. 'Everyone calls me Greg . . . even my mum.' He gave a nervous little smile.

Neil didn't seem to have heard him. 'Here you are at last. I want you to do me a favour.'

A strange terror darted in and out of Greg's head. He couldn't think straight. He started to gabble. 'I'm late. I've got to go home. Sorry.'

Then he began to run.

No one was following him, but he ran all the way home. He fumbled about, trying to put his key in the lock. He could hardly get his breath.

'Hello, love,' his mum called out.

He managed to splutter, 'Hello,' then fell upstairs and on to his bed. He lay there gasping. Suddenly, he picked up his case and hurled it against the wall. 'You've caused all this,' he cried.

Now his mum was calling up the stairs. 'Everything all right, love?'

'Fine, Mum, just dropped something.'

'Did you have a nice day?'

'Yes thanks.'

12

'I've made a pot of tea.'

'I'll be right down,' he said.

'You've got a visitor,' went on Mum. 'He never forgets, does he?'

'No, he never forgets,' said Greg as his cat, Sid, appeared in the doorway. Like most cats, Sid regularly went roaming. But he was always home when Greg returned from school, always waiting for him.

'You're better than any dog, aren't you?' Sid was jet black with piercing yellow eyes. Greg hugged his cat. He was still shaking. Only now he was shaking with anger – at himself. He shouldn't have torn off like that. He'd been silly and cowardly. But it was as if there'd been static inside his head and all he could hear was his own panic.

His running off was like Eric squealing: it only drew attention to Greg and made him seem weak and feeble: it was like laying out bait.

Greg slept badly that night. Every time he thought of tomorrow he felt sick.

Josh had to get out. He had garbled some rubbish to his mum and taken off. He couldn't spend another second in that house, not with the alien settled in it.

That's what he and Lucy called their brand new

step-dad. They'd never liked him, a small, neat, fussy man who wore V-neck sweaters with diamond patterns all over them. Josh had been certain this man was a complete non-starter. He was just someone for Mum to go round with until a better prospect turned up.

Sometimes he'd try to make jokes. So when Lucy asked Mum for an increase in her pocket money, he piped up, 'Pocket money isn't index-linked to inflation, you know.'

Josh and Lucy pretended to find this screamingly funny. Their mum was smiling too: tragically, she really did think his joke was funny.

Their mum was well and truly 'loved-up'. Josh knew all the symptoms. So when his mum said to him and Lucy, 'I've got some exciting news for you both', Josh knew what she was going to say right away.

It was still horrible, though. The day after the honeymoon, Josh and Lucy were sent to the shops to get some extra milk. They walked back really slowly, until finally they were hardly moving at all. They were both laughing very loudly but then Lucy was sobbing as well. Josh took her to the park and let her cry: great, angry sobs. Josh felt angry too. Their whole life was being turned upside down and there was nothing they could do about it. They were just being pulled along like fish on a line.

He resolved to look out for Lucy. Actually, he always had. Whenever Lucy was upset, like that time, ages ago now, when the girls in her class told her she had wobbly knees, it was to Josh she turned. Now Lucy was thirteen and becoming quite pretty. Kane, a boy in Josh's class, was mad about her. He kept sending messages to her via Josh. Lucy thought the whole thing was hilarious. She'd got quite a few admirers and she'd started hanging about with a gang who were all older than her. Josh went out with them sometimes, just to check them out. Lucy knew he was doing this and she teased him about it. But she was pleased too. 'At least someone cares who I see,' she said.

Tonight she'd gone with her friends to the cinema to see 'Giant Eyelashes from Mars', or something terrible like that. So Josh was wandering about on his own. (Andy lived miles away in an even smaller village than this one.) He had planned to buy some fish and chips but in the end he just kept on walking aimlessly. He couldn't bear to go home. He began thinking about that room – his and Andy's room. Of course it didn't belong to them. Other anti-bullying counsellors were supposed to use it too but they'd soon get bored. No kid was going to pop in there and spill out his problems.

Still, he and Andy could make something of the room: maybe decorate it, bring in some decent chairs, a CD player. He could tell Desert Head music would help relax the callers . . .

He was thinking so hard he didn't see a girl rushing out of the village hall. He bumped into her, sending the papers she was carrying flying.

'Oh, no!' she exclaimed.

'I'll get them. No problemo,' cried Josh, energetically scooping up all the papers. 'There you go. I'm not sure if they're in the right order.' He gazed down at one of the pages. It was a script.

'That's all right. Don't worry. I should have stapled them together anyway.' She took the pages from him. She was quite small but she had large, soulful eyes and long black hair. She was wearing green dangly earrings which matched her green eyes.

Josh smiled at her. 'That was a script, wasn't it?'

'That's right.'

'Are you an actress, then?'

She liked that question, Josh could tell. 'Well, sort of . . . I'm with the Christie Players.'

Josh nodded as if he knew them well.

'And I've just got a part in their new play . . . a really good part, actually.'

'Well done.'

'Thanks. I never thought I'd get it.'

'Have you done much acting before?'

'Only small roles, nothing like this. I've been in a few school productions of course.'

'What school do you go to?'

'Mary Aitken.'

'What a very nice school,' said Josh with undisguised sarcasm. Mary Aitken and Havering Boys' schools were the two schools in the area which had excellent reputations. Pupils who wished to attend these 'centres of excellence' had to sit an exam first.

'Actually, some days it's a pain there,' she said. 'There's always some teacher checking you for jewellery or make-up or making sure your grey skirt is exactly the right length. What school do you go to?' she added.

'The local borstal.'

She looked startled.

'Westheath. We don't have a uniform so our teachers' only worry is whether we should be allowed to wear ripped jeans or not.' There was a bitterness in his voice which surprised him. He quickly changed the subject. 'What's the play you're in, then?'

'*A Taste of Honey*. I don't suppose you know it?'

She sounded so hopeful he had to say, 'Yes, of course.'

'I'm playing Jo. My name's Ally, by the way.'

He smiled at her. He really liked her. 'Josh,' he grinned. He was very tempted to ask her out. Instead there was a bit of an awkward silence.

'Well, I'd better go,' she said at last.

He should ask to see her again but he couldn't. What if she said no. The embarrassment would stay with him for weeks. He dug into his pocket for one of the cards he'd had made in London, as a joke. The card had his name, address and telephone number on it and under his name, 'Purveyor of Fine Wit'.

He thrust the card into her hand. 'In case you ever want any help learning your lines,' he said.

Next morning, Greg left home half an hour early. He told his parents there was a special meeting he didn't want to miss. They looked pleased and he heard his dad say, 'Maybe Westheath isn't so bad after all.'

Greg planned to be safely in his classroom before Neil arrived. Soon Neil would forget all about him and move on to someone else. Greg was walking quickly now but he still managed to read his Sherlock Holmes book as well.

Suddenly a tremor ran along his arm. It was like a warning. Greg lowered his book slowly as if it were very heavy. Neil was just ahead of him. He was leaning on the school gates, headphones on, seemingly intent on his music.

A chill seemed to fall across Greg. He thought he'd been so clever sneaking in early. But maybe Neil was waiting for someone else. He had to be. Of what interest could Greg be to him? He walked slowly towards him.

Neil was wearing the same black jersey as yesterday. He didn't look up and he spoke out of the corner of his mouth, as if he were a spy passing on secret information. 'You weren't very friendly yesterday, Gregory.'

'No, I'm sorry. I was in a bit of a rush.'

'But you're early today.' It was no coincidence Neil was here. He'd anticipated what Greg would try to do.

Neil stretched out his hand. 'Let me take your case for you.'

'It's all right. Thanks all the same.'

'But I'd like to. It's so flash.' The next moment he'd snatched at it but Greg was still hanging on too.

'Let go,' murmured Neil. This wasn't a request. It was a command. Neil was looking right at Greg. His pale, starey eyes never seemed to blink. Greg loosened his grip. 'I will need that case . . .' he began. Another boy was hovering. He'd appeared out of nowhere. Neil suddenly threw the case to the boy. He caught it easily and darted away.

'Hey, stop.' Greg turned to Neil. 'Where's he gone with my case?'

Neil shrugged his shoulders.

'But that's my case. He can't just take it.'

'Why not?' said Neil softly. 'Don't worry, you'll get it back . . . eventually.'

'But it's got all my homework in it.'

'Has it now? Still, it's far too early for school yet.' He turned and walked away.

Greg hovered outside his form room, expecting Neil to appear with the case before registration. When he didn't Greg panicked and raced round the school, desperately searching for him. At registration Greg was told off for being late and a few minutes later he received his first-ever detention, for not handing in his geography homework. Greg borrowed a pen and some paper from Steve, the boy he'd been chatting to about Leicester City after football yesterday. Steve let him share his geography textbook. But the geography teacher asked Greg to stay behind at the end of the lesson. 'I'm disappointed in you, Greg, not a very good start, is it?'

Greg hung his head. For a moment he was tempted to tell the teacher that his case had been stolen – but he knew he could never ever do that. He'd be branded a grass and a sneak forever and Neil would take his revenge.

At breaktime, Greg went in search of Neil. There must be a reason why Neil wanted the case. There always was in the Sherlock Holmes stories. Finally Greg decided that Neil wasn't well-off, so he was taking his revenge against people he saw flaunting their wealth – like Greg. Greg must tell him the truth. Then he saw him. He was talking to another boy who Greg vaguely recognised as being in the second year. The boy handed Neil some kind of package then ran off.

'Where's my case?' demanded Greg.

'You won't get anything if you talk in that kind of voice.' Neil's tone was reproving, like a teacher.

'I'm sorry,' he blurted out, 'I'm not rich, you know.

My parents had to save up for that case. Both my mum and dad work and I've got a younger brother. He's only two, well nearly three, and it's a bit of a struggle for us . . .'

Neil just stared at him with his unblinking eyes.

'So, please, can I have my case back? I need it.'

'Sorry. No. You're not ready yet.' He spoke regretfully, yet firmly. 'I will be in contact.'

Greg stared after him. He was joined by Steve. Greg explained what had happened. He could sense Steve becoming more and more uneasy. 'You don't want to tangle with him,' said Steve at last. 'I've heard he's big trouble.'

But Greg hadn't volunteered for this situation – he'd been pulled into it. He asked Steve what he should do.

'Do nothing,' said Steve gravely. 'Wait for him to talk to you.'

Contact was made right at the end of the school day. A map was stuck on to Greg's locker, a crudely drawn map of the school. The chemistry lab, which was right at the top of the school, was marked with an arrow. Greg shot up the four flights of stairs half-expecting to see Neil waiting for him, but no one was about. Greg went over to the first chemistry lab. His case wasn't in there. He peered frantically into the other rooms. It wasn't in any of those either. He was really panicking now. Then he felt a hand on his shoulder. 'Looking for this?' Mrs Withers, the lab technician, was holding his case.

'Oh, yes, yes,' gasped Greg.

'I don't know,' said Mrs Withers, 'you boys would lose your heads if they weren't screwed on.'

'Thank you, thank you,' cried Greg.

He ran down the stairs again. The school was deserted. Those boys on the mopeds he'd seen yesterday weren't around. Neither was Neil. Greg crouched down and opened his case. He couldn't believe what he saw.

He took out a piece of his shatterproof ruler. It had been snapped into three equal bits. Each pencil had been broken in half. So had his pen, the expensive one his parents had bought him. His rubber must have been cut with a knife, it was in tiny pieces. Every one of his exercise books was ripped up and every text book, their remains littering the bottom of the case. Nothing had been spared. It must have taken Neil ages and ages. And then he'd carefully put everything back in its rightful place again. But why? He wasn't even around to savour Greg's misery.

Greg kept taking things out of his case and looking at them until he suddenly jumped up and tipped the entire contents of his case into a metal bin. He shuddered as he did it. Then he began to walk home. He tried to take his mind off what had happened. He stared into a shop window but he didn't see anything except the reflection of what was over the road . . . the cemetery.

All at once he darted across there. He went in and chucked his briefcase into the first bin he found. He couldn't keep it any longer. He knew his parents would be upset, but it was just causing too much hassle. He stepped back. His case looked odd lying there on its side amongst all the withered flowers. It was just as if he were burying it and it was only fourteen days old. It had never had a chance to get scratched or torn or . . . He rushed forward and hauled the case out of its grave. So what if it was a bit swanky, a bit sad? SO WHAT? It was a free country, wasn't it?

Later, he lay on his bed thinking about the day's events. Today Neil had taken his revenge. He would move on to someone else now. It was all over.

Greg kept chanting this to himself. 'It's all over.'

But he couldn't quite believe it.

Two

The next day, Greg slipped into school without apparently being seen by Neil. He was the first one in his form room. There was a message on his desk. It said, simply: BE HERE AT BREAKTIME. There was another map. It pointed to the huts. Greg dreaded another encounter but he daren't ignore this instruction.

The huts were at the back of the school, close to the fence by the road. The windows were cracked (one of them was boarded up) and the walls were covered in graffiti. Teachers hated using them as much as the pupils. The headmaster told the first years that these huts were only temporary. Apparently he told the first years this every year. The huts were raised from the ground. Mounds of litter gathered underneath them.

Neil was sitting on the top step of one hut. He had his headphones on. He appeared to be alone. When he saw Greg he gave one of his half-smiles. He always smiled like someone who needed to practise more.

Greg burst out, 'My case. You destroyed everything. I've been in big trouble with the teachers and I've had to buy all these new pens and pencils . . .'

Neil slowly removed his headphones. 'I really didn't want it to happen,' he said sadly. 'But you brought it on yourself, you know.'

'How?' cried Greg indignantly.

'By your behaviour. Now you've learned a hard lesson, haven't you? You will never run away from me again.' He paused, 'Will you?'

'No, all right, but still . . .'

'No, Gregory, listen. I was kind to you. I carried your case for you. You re-paid my courtesy with rudeness. You made me look foolish in front of my friends. You are in my debt, aren't you?'

Greg nodded slowly. Neil was talking nonsense and yet the conviction in his voice was unsettling, hypnotic. 'I won't do it again,' said Greg humbly. Against all logic, part of him did feel as if he'd acted badly. Then, out of the corner of his eye he spotted Eric. He was screaming at Colin Adams, his chief tormentor. On and on he screamed. He'd caught Neil's attention too.

'That's the boy in our class who everyone picks on. He's called Eric.' Even as Greg spoke he hated and despised himself: what he was really saying was, here's someone else for you to target. Forget about me now: go after him.

Neil seemed to consider this for a moment, then said, 'Are you into music as well as books, Gregory?'

'Well, yes, I like some bands,' began Greg.

'That's good,' said Neil softly. 'I really want this CD. They sell them in Smedleys.'

'They sell everything in Smedleys,' said Greg.

'Would you believe I'm banned from their store?' said Neil.

Greg could believe it very easily, but he tried to look suitably shocked.

'Why don't you go in and get the CD for me?'

'Yes, all right,' said Greg.

'Thank you,' replied Neil. He handed Greg a tiny scrap of paper on which was written the name of the CD. 'Bring it to me here tomorrow, before school starts.' He turned away as if the interview was over.

Distinctly embarrassed, Greg called out, 'Excuse me, but what about the money, please?'

Neil turned round. 'There's no money. Don't break your promise, will you?' Then he got up and walked off.

Greg dug into his pocket. He had thirty pounds left from his birthday money. After school, he very reluctantly went to Smedleys and bought Neil the CD.

Next morning he handed it over. But Greg's debt still wasn't paid in full. Neil wanted another CD for his collection. The next day Greg bought that one too. All his birthday money was gone now. When Neil started telling him about the next CD he wanted, Greg interrupted.

'I'm sorry, I haven't got any money left.'

Neil shrugged his shoulders. 'Take it anyway.'

Greg was stunned. 'You mean steal it?'

'I'd snatch it myself, only I'm a wanted man in that shop – but you're not. You could slip in there very easily and I really want that CD.'

'Look, I got you those other two CDs,' began Greg. 'Used up all my money, too.'

'And now I want another one. I'm a music-lover you see. Go on, it won't take you a minute.' His voice was low and coaxing.

'No, no,' cried Greg. 'I won't do it.'

He looked around him. Suddenly they weren't alone. Two boys were hovering. Greg had seen those boys with Neil before. 'Just leave me alone, all right?' he cried.

Then he ran for his life.

Not one pupil came along to consult the anti-bullying counsellors. The other counsellors quickly lost interest, as Josh had predicted. The absence of callers suited Josh and Andy just fine. It meant there was more coffee and biscuits for them. Mr Denton had remained true to his word, donating a kettle, a jar of coffee, some powdered milk and a huge box of biscuits.

'Now that's what I call a proper box of biscuits,' said Andy. 'Four layers.'

'Don't eat all the good ones,' said Josh, who was selecting a tape to play on his music centre.

'Denton bought all this stuff himself, you know.'

'That man is a saint,' said Josh, 'and a total mug. He believes everything I tell him. He thinks we're solving six problems at this very moment. I keep asking his advice. He loves it when I do that.'

There was a knock on the door.

'The man himself,' said Josh, turning the music

down. Then he and Andy sprang behind their desk. There was nothing on it except a library copy of *A Taste of Honey* which Josh had been reading.

In walked instead a small boy with ginger hair. He planted himself in front of them and demanded, 'Are you the people who can stop bullying?'

Josh raised an eyebrow at the boy's shrill voice and self-important manner. For a moment he was in shock. A real customer. He quickly recovered. 'Yes, that's right, do sit down and tell us how we can help you. Perhaps you would like a cup of coffee?'

The boy shook his head.

'Or a biscuit?'

'I think we've got some ginger nuts left,' said Andy. Josh smothered a giggle.

'Yes, I will have a biscuit,' said the boy.

Andy handed the box to him, the boy studied its contents gravely, then finally made his selection.

'Sure you won't have a coffee?' asked Andy. 'Make your hair curl.' His shoulders shook while he spoke. The boy didn't seem to hear this.

'My name is Eric Smythe and I'm being bullied constantly and I want it to stop.'

'Of course you do,' said Josh.

'You see, I've got ginger hair,' declared Eric.

'My goodness, so you have,' said Josh in mock-amazement. Andy's shoulders were still shaking.

'And everyone keeps calling me Ginger Tom.'

'Ginger Tom,' repeated Josh. He didn't trust himself to look at Andy now.

'Whenever I walk into a classroom, they start chanting it and this goes on all day. Everyone does it, but one boy's the ringleader, he's called Colin Adams. Are you going to write that name down?'

'I certainly am,' said Josh. 'Only I haven't got a pen. Have you got a pen, Andy?'

'No,' spluttered Andy.

'You just can't get the help these days. Don't worry, I've got a brilliant memory. I'll remember that name for the rest of my days. Do carry on. What was the name again?'

'Colin Adams.'

Josh tapped his head. 'It's stored away now, do continue with your very shocking story.'

'Colin Adams keeps running into me and knocking against me. I tell him to stop and leave me alone, but he won't. And he just keeps on taunting me: "Ginger Tom, Ginger Tom." He paused and looked at Josh expectantly.

'Well, this is a grave situation,' said Josh. 'It seems

to be your gingerness which is causing the problem, so have you ever thought of . . . shaving your head?'

At this Andy exploded into laughter and Eric shot to his feet. 'You're just like all the others,' he squeaked. 'You think it's just a big joke. Well it's not, it's . . .'

Josh immediately became serious. 'Eric, Eric, you misunderstand. My colleague here and I were not laughing at you. No, we were just using a little reverse psychology, trying to get you to laugh at your problem and see it in its true perspective . . .'

Andy wondered how Josh could speak complete gibberish and yet sound so plausible and persuasive. Eric had sat down again and was staring intently at Josh, drinking in every word.

'So, what we say to you, Eric,' went on Josh, 'is wear your ginger hair with pride. Will you do that?'

Eric nodded solemnly.

'And this boy . . .'

'Colin Adams,' prompted Eric.

'Send this Colin Adams to us,' said Josh. 'And we guarantee he will never bully you again.'

'I'll get him now,' said Eric rushing to the door.

'That's fine,' said Josh. 'And Eric, you walk with confidence, all right?'

'I will,' said Eric. 'And thank you,' he added humbly.

After he'd gone, Andy and Josh fell about laughing. 'All that garbage you were feeding him about reverse psychology,' said Andy. 'And he swallowed every word.'

'People will believe anything, if you say it with enough conviction. That's the trick.'

'So when this Colin Adams character turns up, what are you going to do? Give him five strokes of the cane?'

'Oh, I'll just tell him to lay off Ginger Tom a bit, that's all,' said Josh casually.

But Colin Adams didn't turn up. 'He says you haven't got any power over him,' declared Eric. 'He says you're not teachers, you're not even prefects. And he's going to get me for reporting him,' he added miserably.

Suddenly the whole situation wasn't quite so amusing. Josh was particularly indignant. 'Colin Adams will see what power we've got.'

Josh sprang off to see Mr Denton who brought Colin Adams along to them himself. But Colin Adams still didn't regard the anti-bullying counsellors as anything very important. He wandered in yawning, wearing his baseball cap round the wrong way and sat down.

'Who gave you permission to sit down?' demanded Josh. 'Stand up.'

Andy darted forward and grabbed Colin Adams's baseball cap and started wiping the window with it.

'Hey, stop that,' the boy cried.

'Shut it,' snapped Josh, really warming to his role. 'Any more of your lip and you'll be sitting on the floor.'

'Like to see you try and make me,' snapped Colin Adams.

'Would you?' said Josh slowly. 'All right, you may sit down now.'

Colin sat down, folded his arms, then sighed loudly. Josh had given the same performance with teachers many times himself. It was only now he realised how irritating it was.

Josh leaned forward and stared at Colin. Andy threw the baseball cap on the floor and resumed his place at the end of the table. He did some eyeballing too. 'We've been asked by the staff to investigate bullying and your name has been put before us,' said Josh at last.

Colin sniggered.

'Our sources tell us,' went on Josh relishing his new role, 'that you've been causing a certain person a lot of grief. What do you have to say about this, Adams?'

'It's not just me,' he began.

'Do you deny the charge?' asked Josh.

'No one likes Ginger Tom. Everyone makes fun of him. You can't just pick me out.'

Josh leaned back in his chair. 'Would you like a cup of coffee?'

Surprised, Colin Adams said, 'Yeah, all right.' While Andy made the coffee, Josh suddenly hissed, 'Why do you think you're so much better than Eric?'

Shocked by this sudden attack, Colin wasn't quite sure what to say.

'How would you like it if I made fun of your hair? You're losing your hair already, aren't you?'

'No!' He was indignant, but panicked too.

'You'll be bald by the time you're twenty. Maybe that's why you make fun of Eric. You're jealous of him.'

'Leave it out.' Colin Adams gave an uneasy laugh.

'Perhaps you're not so perfect yourself, Adams.' This time the boy didn't say anything at all, he just sat studying his trainers. There was a pause. Colin slowly looked up again. Josh was glaring at him. He was staring at Colin as if he were his deadliest enemy. Then in a low, chilling voice, 'We want you to leave Eric alone. If you don't, well, whatever you do to him, we'll do six times worse to you. And that's a promise. Now get out of our sight.'

Colin Adams fled without saying another word, without even retrieving his baseball cap.

As soon as he'd left, that grave, solemn figure behind the desk started jumping round the room with Andy. They were both waving their fists in the air like triumphant football supporters.

'Did you see his face?' cried Andy. 'He was really bricking it. I bet he's gone off to change his underpants.'

'And we did it,' said Josh incredulously. 'He took it all, hook, line and sinker. I bet he really does lay off Ginger Tom, too.' Josh was grinning from ear to ear now. 'That was a brilliant crack.'

It was five o'clock on Sunday afternoon. In the kitchen a party was going on: it was for Greg's little brother, David. He was three years old today. Greg wasn't there. He'd fled upstairs. Normally he enjoyed his little brother's parties – three and four year olds could be so funny. Today, though, Greg didn't want to do anything except lie in the dark. He lay there for ages. Finally he switched on his bedside light. He sat up. A face stared back at him in the mirror. A face he hated. He began shouting at it. 'Why, out of everyone in your form, did Neil have to pick on you? It's nothing to do with your briefcase. It's you, you're weak and pathetic.'

He lay back again, remembering the parties his mum and dad had put on for him. Often a boy would come up and grab a toy out of Greg's hand. But he never snatched it back. Why not? Why hadn't he ever fought back? Maybe he was just born feeble.

Greg's head was getting heavier. It was going to burst in a minute. He reached out for his Sherlock Holmes book which luckily he'd kept in his jacket pocket so Neil hadn't destroyed it. He was almost at the end. He read as slowly as he could. He didn't want the story to finish. Afterwards he thought, if only Sherlock Holmes were real, then he could go and consult him. He'd sit in Sherlock Holmes's room beside a roaring fire and Dr Watson would insist Greg had a hot drink. Then Sherlock Holmes would listen really carefully to Greg and afterwards he'd say . . .

Greg thought hard.

Sherlock Holmes would say, 'You must face up to Neil, however difficult, and you mustn't, under any circumstances, steal for him. Is that clear?' It was very clear. And right then Greg felt brave, as if he could do anything. Tomorrow he'd tell Neil where to shove his CDs.

Tomorrow arrived early. Greg didn't usually hear his dad leave for work, but today he did. Then he heard his mum get up and go downstairs. Now she was calling the time up the stairs. Greg should get up. But he couldn't. He couldn't move. All his energy had gone – and all his courage. He lay listening to his little brother singing to himself next door. Finally his mum came charging in. 'Greg, come on. You should have been up ages ago.'

'Don't feel too good, Mum.' She felt his forehead and asked about his symptoms. Moments later she returned with a thermometer and took his temperature.

'You're really not ill, are you, love?' she said quietly, confidingly.

Greg felt ashamed. He turned away from her. She sat down on the bed. 'Anything wrong at school?'

Should he tell her? He wanted to very much. But he knew she'd be upset and insist on marching up to the school. He shuddered. His parents were great, but like all parents they over-reacted and were about as subtle as a brick.

'I think it's time I visited your school,' went on Mum. She'd never been happy about him going there.

'No, Mum. No. Nothing's wrong. I just didn't fancy going to school today.'

She laughed, half-reassured. 'Got the Monday morning blues, have you?'

'That's it,' said Greg, stumbling out of bed.

She paused at the door. 'You would tell me if anything was bothering you?'

'Yes, Mum, of course.'

Greg spent the day at school constantly looking over his shoulder. He went round with Steve whenever he could. They both put their names down to try out for the school football team. He didn't eat anything at lunchtime – he just wasn't hungry – and spent the whole time in the library reading *The Memoirs of Sherlock Holmes*.

He left school relieved. He hadn't seen Neil all day. He hoped that Neil now realised that Greg couldn't be pushed around. This time, Neil had targeted the wrong person. He was walking out of the gates when a boy came up to him. Greg recognised

39

him, he had given Neil the package last week. He smiled companionably.

'It's Gregory, isn't it?'

'Greg.'

'Well, I'm Mike.' He stretched out his hand. It seemed an oddly formal greeting. Next Mike gave a peculiar giddy laugh and said, 'You live on the edge, don't you?'

Greg looked puzzled.

'Neil's not best pleased with you, says you've let him down.'

'I haven't let him down. I just refused to steal a CD for him.'

'Why?'

'Why?' Greg was taken aback by the question. 'Because . . .' he lowered his voice. 'Well, it's not right, is it?'

Mike gave another giddy laugh. 'Rather you than me.' Then he added, 'You know we're being watched, don't you?' He nodded at a boy standing across the road. A boy whose face was shaped a bit like a potato. His eyes were small and dark. He wasn't very big but there was something scary about him all the same. Maybe it was his look of sour misery.

'That's Phil, one of Neil's deputies. Neil's got a

lot of deputies in this school, and beyond.'

'But why's he watching us?' asked Greg.

'You, actually,' said Mike. 'Take my tip, nip into Smedleys and pick up the CD. It won't take you a second and then all your worries will be over.'

'Until he wants another CD.'

'But that might not be for weeks,' said Mike. 'Neil's a fair man if you keep on the right side of him. Go on, no one ever gets caught nicking in Smedleys.'

'Well, Neil obviously did as he's banned from there,' said Greg, sounding braver than he felt. 'Thanks for the advice but I'm not stealing anything.'

'All right.' Mike smiled regretfully. 'Let me know where to send the wreath, won't you?'

Greg didn't appreciate that last crack. He also decided he didn't like Mike very much, for all his pretend friendliness. Had Mike been acting as a messenger for Neil? Was this a kind of final warning?

It was good to get home and shut the door on all that craziness. He went up to play on his computer. To his surprise, Sid wasn't waiting for him. 'He's let me down today,' said Greg jokingly. At six o'clock Sid still wasn't home and Greg was starting to get anxious. He and his mum went out in the car to look for him. There was no sign. Greg popped round to the neighbours: sometimes Sid honoured one of them with a visit.

But no one had seen him today.

Greg's dad came home. He told them to stop fussing: cats were always roaming off. He'd be back when he was hungry. But Greg was convinced Sid was lying injured somewhere. All thoughts of Neil had swept out of his head. He had to find his cat.

He went out again. The night air felt sharp and cold. It was the first really chilly autumn night. He walked for miles. On his way home a car stopped. It was his dad. They drove around. Greg couldn't stop shivering. His dad turned the heating right up, talking cheerily and loudly of how Sid would soon be back. Then he switched the radio on, a football match. Usually Greg and his dad could chat about football for hours. Tonight they drove home in silence.

When they got home it was after ten o'clock, past Greg's bedtime. Greg refused to go to bed. Sid had been his cat since he was two years old, he had to wait up for him now. His parents hovered, uncertain what to do. 'We can't do much now,' said Greg's mum gently. 'But first thing tomorrow, I'll put some notices round and we'll offer a reward.'

Everything was becoming more and more hopeless. Sid was lying dead somewhere, he knew it.

The doorbell rang. Then Greg heard his mum exclaim, 'Oh, you've found him.' Greg flew to the door where he saw a familiar figure holding Sid in his arms. Cold waves ran up and down his back.

Neil was saying, 'I thought I'd better bring him back because . . . well, anything could happen to him.'

'It's so good of you to take the trouble to find us,' said Greg's mum.

'It's no trouble.' Then he said, 'Oh, hello, it's Gregory, isn't it? I know you from school, don't I?'

Greg could only glare at him.

'I'm Neil,' he went on conversationally.

'We're so grateful to you, Neil,' began Greg's mum.

Suddenly Greg lunged forward and snatched his cat out of Neil's arms. Then he turned his back on Neil. Greg's mum gave a little gasp at her son's brusqueness.

'He's been very anxious about his cat,' she explained. 'Been his pet since he was two.'

'I quite understand,' said Neil. But his eyes remained as blank and empty as ever. 'And I'm so pleased your cat is safe again, Gregory. Goodbye.'

Greg's mum closed the door with a contented sigh. 'Well don't stand there frowning, Greg. You've got Sid back safe and sound. Silly cat wandering off like that. I'm so glad we put a name tag on him otherwise . . . well, I don't know what would have happened. I suppose he would have found his way back eventually.' She rubbed Sid's head affectionately, then said, 'I think this calls for a pot of tea.'

Greg heard his parents talking while Sid lay purring in his arms. He was a cat who liked to be fussed over. But Greg stood staring out of the window. He shivered. Cold air had started creeping in through the glass. Then he heard someone whistling loudly, tunelessly. He was sure it was Neil.

Later that night he woke up with a jump. He sat upright, sweat pouring down his forehead. He was sure he could still hear Neil whistling.

Each night Josh was on phone-alert, waiting for Ally to call. A week went by. Then she did ring. She had a play rehearsal. Would he care to meet up at the café nearby afterwards? She spoke really fast. He could hardly catch what she was saying.

He waited outside the café for her. He stamped his feet because he was cold and nervous. She looked dead nervous too. This was quite a posh café. They were shown to a table. In the middle of it was a vase with a sickly-looking yellow rose in it. He and Ally kept sneaking glances at the ailing flower. It seemed like a bad omen. It put him off.

They ordered two coffees. That bit was okay, but then they started struggling. Josh felt self-conscious and awkward. She looked gorgeous, though. Every night he'd lain awake picturing her. Now, here he was sitting across a table from her, and floundering. Then she said: 'I was really surprised you knew *A Taste of Honey*.'

'Were you?'

'Yes. I mean, it's a play about a mother and daughter, and some boys – well most boys – wouldn't be interested in that.' She spoke as if she were paying him a compliment.

There was his cue. Now he had a part: the eager, sincere boy who is not afraid to express his feelings. He took out his copy of *A Taste of Honey*. He'd read the whole play and the introductory notes. He started talking about it. Her eyes grew wider. He even threw in a few quotes.

'One line I really like,' he spoke enthusiastically, but with a little shy smile, 'is when Jo says to Geoff,

"You're nothing to me. I'm everything to myself." '

Now her eyes were huge. 'How strange you should pick that line . . . it's my favourite from the whole play.'

'It is?'

'And it gave me the key to Jo's whole character. I mean, her mum's never been around for her, nor has anyone else. She's got no one to turn to. She's completely alone.' Then she said again, 'How strange you should pick that particular line too.'

Josh had certainly served up an ace that time.

There was no stopping Ally now. 'The thing I like best about acting is finding out about people, discovering what makes them tick and making connections between them and ourselves . . . that's what Veronica Lambert, our drama teacher, says we've got to keep doing, making connections.'

'Do you want to be an actress, then?'

'So many people say that, don't they?' She gave a rueful smile. 'But just as soon as I can, I want to put myself through acting college.'

'I think you'll make it,' said Josh suddenly.

'Why?'

'I don't know. It's just a feeling I've got.' Josh was only spinning her a line, telling her what she wanted to hear. And yet he could picture her as an actress. For a start she had a good voice and he supposed that was one of the most important things of all. She spoke slightly breathlessly – but she had a strong, warm tone. You could imagine that voice reading a bedtime story on the radio. Josh would tune in all right.

She leaned over. 'Right, I want to know about you – and your family, now.'

'Well my dad's in the circus.' Then he grinned at her startled face. 'No, nothing so interesting. My dad's in South Africa.'

'Doing what?'

'I couldn't tell you. He walked out when I was five, never seen him since. So that left my mum, my sister Lucy and me – and, oh yes, recently we've had a new addition to the clan called a step-dad.'

'And what's he like?'

'Well, my mum met him through a dating agency.' Josh made a face.

'But that's all right. I mean, loads of people go to them now.'

'I'd rather take poison,' said Josh. 'They're just too sad for words.'

'But if people find happiness through them?'

Realising he was tarnishing his caring-and-in-touch-with-his-emotions image, Josh conceded, 'You could be right but then I must tell you, my step-dad wears a plum-coloured suit.'

'Oh, that is worrying.'

'He's so grim, Ally, you wouldn't believe it. I mean, he and my mum got hitched at this registry office-do in August. Afterwards my step-dad went and wrapped up all the pieces of cake that were left and stuffed them into his bag.'

'That's so tacky.'

'I know, but what's worse, he did this in full view of my mum. I was certain she'd ask for an immediate divorce. Instead, she joined in.'

'It must be horrible having him in the house all the time,' said Ally, smiling sympathetically.

'The other day I wandered into the kitchen to find my mum and the alien together, snogging. I felt a right gooseberry.'

'I'm not surprised. So you don't get on with your step-dad, then?'

'I don't.' Josh was very tempted to tell her about something that had happened last Saturday. He had been in the garage doing up a go-cart for Lucy's birthday when his step-dad burst in and yelled at Josh for making a mess and using his tools without permission . . . Josh was too stunned to reply at first. Then suddenly he yelled back at his step-dad, these were not his tools and this was not his garage, and what Josh did was nothing to do with him. Josh became quite hysterical. In fact, for a few moments, he totally lost it. Finally, his step-dad just walked away.

Josh spent the rest of the afternoon in the garage. He didn't come out until he heard his mum and sister return from town. Then he thought there'd be an almighty hassle. But his step-dad didn't say a word about what had happened. He kept giving Josh these really cold stares, though.

Josh didn't care. He was very happy to stay out of his step-dad's way. He just wished he hadn't lost control like that. He felt ashamed of himself. That's why he didn't even tell his sister about it. And finally, he decided not to tell Ally. He didn't want to shatter her image of him.

So he said quickly, 'Lucy and I despise him, but we're hardly in the house these days. She's always out with this gang. I've met them. They're all right . . . and I keep very busy.'

Then he went on to a much more interesting topic

– him becoming an anti-bullying counsellor. He told her about Eric, not adding that so far Eric had been his only client. She was hugely impressed.

'You know, you're so different to what I'd imagined. I mean, when I first met you, I never guessed you were so deep.'

Josh suspected he was about as deep as a puddle, but he gave another sheepish smile.

'And you actually care about people, don't you?'

Josh lowered his eyes modestly. The conversation was just bubbling along now. Even that yellow rose seemed to have perked up. Josh insisted on walking Ally home.

'This is my road,' said Ally. 'I'm four doors down.'

Josh launched into his patter again. 'Well, I've really enjoyed this evening.' Then he stopped. Someone was whistling. Someone was sitting on the wall opposite Ally's house and whistling tunelessly.

It was Neil. Of all the people from his form it would be that spooky sicko. He and Josh weren't exactly enemies, Neil was one person Josh didn't want as an enemy. But Josh didn't like Neil at all. Josh wrinkled up his face in disgust then he realised he was being scrutinised by Ally.

'This isn't where you pictured me living, is it?'

'What? . . . Oh, no,' he cried, genuinely horrified that she would think he was some sort of snob.

'You imagined me living somewhere much posher, didn't you?' She was smiling but she wasn't amused.

'Look, don't be silly.' But she wasn't convinced. The evening had been going so well, he had to get it back. If only that whistling would stop.

Now she was gabbling on again. 'Money's a bit tight at the moment. You see, my dad was made redundant two years ago and he's only recently got a new job. But he has to work nights. My mum works too, at the college, with people who have learning difficulties.' She was talking even faster than she had on the phone.

'I don't want to hear all this,' he shouted. 'I mean, I do want to know everything about you, but . . .' He was sure the whistling was getting even louder. 'But I don't care about where you live.'

She looked at him. 'You seem so different now.'

'No, I'm the same. Honestly. It's just . . .' Should he tell her that he knew the boy sitting on the wall whistling and that he was putting him right off, giving him stage fright in fact? He decided he would. He lowered his voice. 'Would you believe, that guy over there is in my form?'

'You mean Neil? Oh, he lives opposite.'

'He does?' He wasn't sure why he was so shocked. Totally thrown now, he tried to change the subject again. 'It's been great meeting you and talking about plays,' but his voice wasn't right, it was too formal, too self-conscious. 'And I know you'll make a brilliant Jo in *A Taste of Honey*.'

But this time his flattery went straight into the net.

She turned away from him. 'I've got to go in now.'

'Yeah, right . . . I'll give you a ring.'

'You don't have to.'

'I want to,' he replied.

She didn't answer. Not even a smile. He set off home.

'All right, Josh?' called a voice from across the road.

Josh gritted his teeth. 'All right, Neil.' At this moment he hated the guy's guts. He'd ruined tonight and Josh was certain he knew it. Then Josh heard Neil calling Ally's name. Josh turned round. Ally and Neil, their faces in shadow, were talking together.

Next morning, there was no sign of Neil. Greg was

relieved, and yet he wasn't. He knew he was going to come across Neil again and part of him wanted to get it over with. He hated this waiting. He felt sick. He felt as if he'd swallowed a large ball and he couldn't budge it. It just lay there inside his stomach.

At times he could hardly breathe. One of the teachers asked him if he was all right. He should have said no, then he could have gone home. Only Neil had been to his home so nowhere was safe from him.

At lunchtime he was standing in the queue when Phil came and stood next to him. 'Neil wants to see you. Now,' he said.

Greg left the queue right away and followed him. Greg could guess where they were going. He was being taken to Neil's turf: the huts. Only today, Phil walked straight into one of the huts. He didn't invite Greg inside. In fact, he closed the door in Greg's face. One of the teachers must have forgotten to lock the door or maybe Neil had forced the lock. Two boys stood staring at Greg. Were they more of Neil's deputies? Greg wondered just how many deputies he had.

The door opened again. 'Go in,' said Phil. Neil was sitting with his feet on the teacher's table. He had a lighter in his hand which he kept flicking on and off. Greg walked towards him, but Neil didn't look up, too obsessed by the lighter. On, off. On, off. He was like a small child playing with a new toy. Finally, reluctantly, Neil looked up. The light caught his face. His eyes were puffy and his skin was more pasty than ever. He looked washed out: not really scary, except for the peculiar blankness of his gaze.

'I didn't feed your cat yesterday,' he whispered. 'Hope you didn't mind. But it's so difficult to know what cats eat, and I didn't want him getting sick.'

'You're the one who's sick,' burst out Greg angrily. Then he immediately faltered. He'd gone too far. But Neil didn't seem to object at all.

'Yes, I am sick,' he replied. 'So what? But I also like the finer things in life, just like you.'

Greg wasn't certain how to reply to that.

Neil suddenly put the cigarette lighter down. 'Gregory . . .' he began. Greg had given up telling him that no one else called him by that name. 'Have you ever seen a book you really want and yet you can't have? You can't afford it?'

'Yes,' said Greg cautiously.

'That's how it is with me and music. I see CDs I want, but I can't buy them. So I rely on people who are in my debt, like yourself.' His voice became quite gentle. 'Now, I know it's hard for you to understand that, but I've been good to your family, very good.'

What nonsense, thought Greg. Neil hadn't been good to his family at all. But he sounded so friendly and reasonable, and Greg wanted him to stay like that so he didn't argue.

'Now, Gregory, if you will get me this CD, then I think you will have paid your due to me in full, for a while. I'll leave you and your family in peace.' He said this as though he were granting Greg a special favour and part of Greg couldn't help feeling grateful to Neil for being so kind to him.

'So, all you've got to do is deliver the CD to me, here, before school starts tomorrow, that's all I shall ask.' He was being magnanimous. How could Greg refuse? But he had to.

'Look, I'll have some money next week.' He'd asked his mum for ten pounds that morning. His mum had gone on about his birthday money and surely he hadn't spent it all already. But then she'd softened and said things were a bit tight this week as they'd had to buy special shoes for David to stop his feet turning inwards, but next week she'd see what she could do.

Neil shook his head gravely. 'I must have the CD first thing tomorrow. It's already late.'

'But I can't steal it. I've never stolen anything in my life,' exclaimed Greg. 'I don't agree with stealing.'

Neil gave one of his half-smiles, as if Greg had just made a joke. 'It'll only take you a few seconds – a minute at the most. Just go in and be casual, don't look all round you, grab the CD and walk out again. It's not as if I'm asking you to take anything else.' Neil gave a dry laugh. 'I was in one of these DIY shops once and I watched this man trying to steal some copper pipes for his bathroom. He shoved them down his trouser leg and walked out of the shop with this huge exaggerated limp. That was stupid. He got caught easily. I'd never ask you to do that. Anyway, you'd better go and have your dinner. Goodbye, Gregory, and give my best to your family, won't you? I really enjoyed meeting them – and Sid, of course. You look after him now.'

Greg began to back away. He reached the door.

'Gregory.'

He stopped.

'Don't let me down. Bring it to me here. First thing tomorrow. All right?'

Greg nodded then he walked quickly away. He

could just make it back to the dining room in time.
But he went somewhere quite different.

Three

Greg raised his hand and tapped on the door. Eric had recommended them. He said Colin Adams kept right away from him now. They were Greg's last hope.

No one said 'Come in'. Greg could hear raised voices. Perhaps he should wait a bit. He couldn't wait much longer, though. It was nearly the end of the lunch-hour.

Inside, Andy was shouting. 'Look, you can't just come into Bowling Ally's life . . .'

'Bowling Ally? I knew you'd call her that,' interrupted Josh, 'you're so immature.'

'Look who's talking . . . if I might be permitted to finish.'

'Go on, then.'

'I'm giving you good advice here, but then you don't like taking advice, do you? You just like dishing it out.'

'I'm listening,' cried Josh.

'All right . . . I forget what I was going to say now.' Josh began to laugh. 'Oh, yes, I've remembered. You can't come into Bowling Ally's life and start criticising her friends.'

'You think Neil's a friend of hers, then?' demanded Josh.

'No, you're twisting my words now. He's a neighbour of Bowling Ally's, isn't he? And she'll feel defensive. At the moment you're the outsider, so tread carefully. Don't say anything about Neil yet.' Andy paused. He had a steady girlfriend, while Josh did not. In this one area Andy had the authority.

'Okay, message received and understood,' said Josh. He stared gloomily ahead of him. 'I just wish I could warn her about him.'

'What would you say?'

'That Neil's a total headcase.'

'She'll know that already.'

'I'm not so sure. Last night she seemed very pally with him. For all I know she might even fancy the guy.'

Andy's voice rose incredulously. 'You're telling me that Neil's a babe magnet?'

'How do I know?'

'Come on, even his mum couldn't call him good-looking. He doesn't do anything with himself, wears the same clothes all year. He's not roguish or funny – he's just twisted and girls don't go for that. Certainly not Bowling Ally. She's just being neighbourly.'

'Neighbourly,' echoed Josh.

'Why make such a big deal of Neil, anyway? We hardly ever speak to him. He's just some warped thing in the back of the class. So what if he lives near Bowling Ally – so what . . . ?'

'You're right again, of course,' said Josh. 'Don't forget to send me your bill, exclusive of VAT.'

Andy grinned. 'If you want to know anything more about girls . . . just ask me.'

Josh laughed. Then they both heard the knock on the door.

'Somebody's cutting it a bit fine,' said Andy.

'We don't clock-watch in H.Q.,' said Josh taking up his position. 'Come in, whoever you are.'

'H.Q. Since when has this place been called H.Q?' asked Andy.

'Well, I thought the name had a certain ring to it.'

They were still discussing it when Greg crept inside.

'Come in, sit down,' said Josh, staring curiously at the visitor. The boy looked about the same age as Eric but he was much bigger and there was nothing to mark him out as a victim. He just seemed average, except for a certain intenseness.

'I'm Josh and this is my assistant, Andy. I'm afraid you're a bit late for coffee but wc might have a chocolate biscuit left.'

Greg had missed lunch so he took the biscuit gratefully and started to relax. There was something about this eccentric boy which reminded him of Sherlock Holmes. For the first time Greg allowed himself a little spark of hope. Perhaps these two really could help him. 'I have come to seek your help.' Now he was even talking like one of Sherlock Holmes's clients.

'Seek away,' said Josh breezily.

'I am being . . .' Greg didn't want to say 'bullied', '. . . being bothered by this boy.'

Andy raised an eyebrow but Josh avoided his gaze. He was quite intrigued.

'He has been . . .' Greg hesitated. It was hard to explain.

'Take your time,' said Josh pleasantly, 'and have another chocolate biscuit.'

Greg took a second biscuit. He stared down solemnly and spoke into the biscuit as if it were a microphone. 'This boy has been taking my things. Well, he took my case and hid it in the science block. And then when I got it back, everything in it was cut up: all my pens and rubbers, my books . . .'

'And is this boy in your form?' asked Josh, wondering if this was Colin Adams's handiwork.

'No, he's an older boy called Neil . . .' Both Josh and Andy started. 'I don't know his other name but I think he is in the fourth year and he hangs about by the huts a lot.'

'We know who you mean,' said Andy slowly.

Josh was stunned. Neil, of all people. Josh was now doubly wary of him.

The bell went. Andy immediately jumped up. 'No more time, I'm afraid,' he said.

But Greg didn't move. He just sat staring up at Josh, who said, 'Look, the best advice we can give you is just keep away from Neil. He is a bit of a nutter and . . .'

'And you're going to be late for your lesson,' interrupted Andy.

'Stay right away from Neil,' repeated Josh.

'That's what everyone tells me,' said Greg wearily. He got to his feet slowly. 'Goodbye,' he murmured as he walked to the door.

'Come back tomorrow and we'll talk about it in more detail,' called Josh after him. But Greg didn't seem to hear.

The door had hardly closed before Andy announced, 'We're staying right out of that one.'

Greg sat trembling outside Smedleys. He'd been trembling so violently he'd had to sit down. School children often sat outside Smedleys although Greg never had before. It wasn't very comfortable. His head throbbed. He knew he was being watched. Across the road by the cemetery gates' bus stop was Phil, the boy with a face like a potato. He was leaning casually against the stop. But Greg had never seen him there before. He knew Potato Head was acting as Neil's eyes. And maybe as a reminder to Greg as well.

Greg tried to steady himself. He wasn't sure how to do this. He slowed his breathing down, that helped a little. He dreaded what he had to do. But if he didn't do it . . . Doom was pressing in on him from all angles. He felt very scared, yet he was also boiling with resentment towards Neil, towards his deputies, towards everyone. They'd all let him down.

He'd hoped Josh was going to do something. Greg had been quite impressed by him at first. But as soon as he had uttered Neil's name – well, it was as if he'd said Count Dracula or something. Josh had immediately backed off. No one wanted to tangle with Neil. 'Stay away from him,' they choroused. Greg couldn't stay away. He'd been picked out; he was one of Neil's targets. He was going to have to steal that CD. It would buy him a little time, but he knew Neil would demand more favours. By then, though, Greg would be gone.

Greg had nearly passed the exam to go to Havering Boys' School. He'd missed it by two marks. On the day of the exam he had been recovering from 'flu, so the school had said he could resit. But Greg had foolishly refused. He had been weary of exams and figured he might be happier at an ordinary school. Now, perhaps, he could still sit the exam. He'd ask his parents tonight. But if he couldn't . . . His whole body began to shake again. No. He must be positive. He could escape.

Across the road, Potato Head seemed to be getting impatient. Greg took one last deep breath. This was the first and last time he was ever going to have to do this. He clambered to his feet.

'All you've got to do is steal one little CD.' Greg chanted this to himself. It didn't help. Waves of disgust still swept over him. He hated himself for doing this. Neil would surely have known that too. That was why he'd asked Greg to steal. 'Just go in and be casual, get the CD and walk out again.' Neil's words rang through Greg's head. He stepped inside the shop.

'Why, hello, Greg.'

He nearly jumped out of his skin. The woman behind the counter beamed at him. 'Don't you remember me? Mrs Haylen?'

'Oh, yes, of course, hello.' His mouth was so dry he could hardly speak.

'I didn't recognise you at first, you've grown so much.' Greg tried to smile at her. 'How's your mum?'

'She's fine, thank you.'

'I'm just working here afternoons until . . .'

Four boys trooped in.

Mrs Haylen was on red alert immediately. 'Only two of you in here at a time.' There were groans of protest. 'And if you don't like it, you can all leave now,' she said.

Greg saw his chance. He made his way to the

back of the shop where the CDs lived, alongside the books and the videos. He put down his case. He could hear Mrs Haylen still arguing with the boys while he rifled through the CDs. For an awful moment his mind went blank and he couldn't remember what he was supposed to be stealing. But then the title jumped out at him. He grabbed it.

His hands were as damp as an old nappy. The CD slithered about.

Mrs Haylen had stopped talking. The shop was suddenly silent. Was she watching him? Greg knew he mustn't look round. That would only draw attention to himself. He shoved the CD down his jacket. It still felt slippery. His heart hammering, he began walking out of the shop. What if these CDs were alarmed? Any moment now a bell would start to ring. He reached the door. No bell rang. He opened the door. Then he froze. A hand had clasped his shoulder firmly.

'Greg, stop.' It was Mrs Haylen's voice. She sounded angry.

But Greg didn't stop. Instead, he tore out of the shop and ran blindly into the road. He didn't see the car coming towards him. There was a screech of brakes.

And then Greg didn't see anything at all.

Four

Josh saw the crowd gathering.

Something was wrong. He hated people who stood and gawped at accidents. This was probably some old geezer who'd wandered into the road without looking. He pushed through the crowd. A woman in a grey business suit was waving a mobile phone and exclaiming, 'He just flew out of nowhere. I couldn't have stopped. No one could have stopped.'

'That's true,' declared a red-faced man solemnly. I saw the whole thing from my bedroom window. I saw exactly what happened.'

Josh bent down. He'd been expecting to see someone old. But it was a boy and he knew him. He'd remember his name in a minute. Just a couple of hours earlier, that boy had been sitting in H.Q. Now he was lying there, sprawled in the road, with his eyes closed.

He was alive though, surely. Josh leaned forward.

Greg's eyes fluttered open.

He saw blood trickling down one of his legs. He tried to move it. A terrible pain shot through him. He was trapped. He looked up at a sea of feet and legs. He could hear whispering. They were whispering about him. 'He's a shoplifter.' He was sure he'd heard someone say that.

He wished they'd all go away. He wanted his mum and dad. No he didn't. Because then they'd find out what he'd done. The shame of it all. They wouldn't tell him off, but they'd be so shocked and upset.

Someone kneeled down. A man with a very thick neck. His whole face seemed huge. He was asking Greg how he felt. Greg pretended he didn't understand. He half-closed his eyes and ran his hand over his face. He just wanted to lie there. He opened his eyes again. All those faces seemed to swim in front of him. But then, incredulously, he recognised someone. He let out a gasp which caught somewhere in his throat. It was the boy he'd gone to see.

'Josh,' he yelped in amazement. But how was he here? Josh was crouching down and smiling at him. Greg raised a hand as if trying to signal. 'Help me,' he whispered.

Josh hated everything about hospitals but especially that too-clean smell. It was like a particularly nasty aftershave which he couldn't shake off, not even in the little cubicle where he was now waiting with Greg.

Greg lay on a bed in the casualty unit. A nurse chattered while she took Greg's pulse and blood pressure. 'I'm just letting you know what I'm doing. We'll soon have you sorted out.' She sounded re-assuring, but Josh wondered if she always spoke like that, even if you were due to peg out in twenty seconds. Finally she said, 'Now, the doctor is on his way and we've rung your parents and mentioned you've got your friend here with you.'

'Your friend', that made Josh feel a bit of a fake, especially as it was only in the ambulance he re-membered Greg's name. He'd been surprised – and flattered – that Greg wanted him to come along. But now he was getting into the role. As the nurse was leaving, he asked her in a low voice, 'How bad is he?'

'He's got a nasty gash on his leg and he may have fractured his ankle, so we'll have to keep an eye on him for a little while. But I'm sure he'll be fine. Right now, though, we just need to keep him calm and happy.'

Josh nodded gravely. The nurse left and Josh sat on the chair by Greg's bed.

'Thanks for staying,' said Greg. He looked very pale and dazed.

'No problem.'

There was a question Josh had to ask. He wasn't sure if he should, but he had to know. 'Greg, when you ran into the road, you weren't being chased by anyone – like Neil, for instance?'

'No, I wasn't.'

Inside his head Josh heaved a sigh of relief. If this accident was the result of bullying, Josh would have felt guilty. He still felt bad, though. He and Andy hadn't been much help to Greg today.

Then he noticed Greg was shivering. 'What's the matter? Do you feel worse?' he asked. 'I can get someone.'

'No, no.' Greg looked at Josh and whispered, 'I'm a known shoplifter.' He said this so urgently and dramatically, it sounded corny. Josh and Andy sometimes spoke that way to each other when they were messing about. But tears were coursing down Greg's face. And he was breathing funnily, as if he couldn't get enough air.

Josh felt embarrassed. He tapped Greg's hand. 'Hey, come on. What have you stolen, then?'

Greg dug into his pocket, his hand shaking, and produced a CD.

'Is this it?' Josh nearly laughed out loud.

But Greg was whispering. 'I stole it today and this woman saw me and called my name, that's why I ran . . . and she knows my mum and dad, too.' His voice cracked with shame.

'It's okay,' said Josh, tapping Greg's hand again. He didn't know what else to say. He didn't quite understand this. 'Do you collect this band's CDs then? Is that why you took it?'

'No,' hissed Greg. 'I don't even know who they are. I've never heard of them.'

'But why?' began Josh, then he didn't need to ask any more. 'Neil made you steal this, didn't he?'

Greg began to talk so fast that his words were jumping over themselves. Josh couldn't follow all of it, but he picked up enough. He didn't interrupt Greg once. His heart beat faster and he could feel something rising which felt like sick. Only it was something with an even more bitter taste: shame. And Josh couldn't stop it. It was in his mouth now. The taste made him want to retch. Suddenly he shouted out, 'We messed up big time today.' It was almost like an announcement.

Greg didn't quite understand.

'You came to us for help and we let this happen.'

'But it's not your fault,' croaked Greg. 'It's Neil.' His face became clenched with pain.

'We messed up,' repeated Josh. 'But now I'm going to sort things out.'

'You are?' Greg looked even more dazed than ever.

Josh jumped to his feet. 'Give me the CD, Greg. I'm going to take it back. They won't press charges. They won't tell your parents.'

Greg handed him the CD.

'And this bullying by Neil. It's got to stop. It will. Neil will never bother you again.'

Greg's eyes opened wide now. 'But how . . . ?'

'Just trust me, all right?'

'Yes, I will.'

'Everything's going to be all right,' said Josh. Greg was gazing at him with undisguised admiration, while Josh felt more like himself again.

He walked the two miles back to the shop. He was determined Mrs Haylen wasn't going to report Greg for shoplifting. He'd give her the CD back then he'd play on the violins: hasn't Greg suffered enough? All that stuff. If that didn't work, he'd say the boy ran into the road because of her. She'd frightened him out of his wits . . .

He asked for Mrs Haylen. 'I believe you served Greg . . .'

'Oh, yes, how is he? You're the boy who got into the ambulance with him, aren't you?'

'Well, they're keeping him in,' began Josh. He started telling her about Greg's injuries, only laying it on a bit thick. The woman listened intently to him, sighing sympathetically. Then she said in a rather more business-like voice, 'Well, I know why you are here.'

Josh tensed, ready for a battle.

'And if no one had called round I was going to drop the case off myself after we'd finished here.' She bent down, then handed the briefcase over the counter to Josh. 'Poor lad, I called after him but he walks round in a dream, a lot of the clever ones do, don't they?'

73

Recovering himself now, Josh said, 'It was very kind of you to keep the case. Greg had been so worried about it.'

'He worries too much, that boy. You tell him to concentrate on getting well: health's the most important thing, you know . . .'

Josh rang the hospital. The casualty nurse remembered him and said Greg's parents were there now. They were keeping Greg in over night, but they didn't think he'd fractured his ankle as they'd feared, it was just a very severe sprain and a cut knee. Then she let him have a quick word with Greg.

'I spoke to Mrs Haylen. She says you left that briefcase behind. She tried to tell you . . .'

'My scabby briefcase,' gasped Greg laughing helplessly.

'Becoming a bit of a legend, that case, isn't it? And I'm working on that other little problem now.'

That night anger crashed in on Josh. He thought of Greg lying in a hospital bed. The torture he'd been put through these last weeks. And all because of Neil and that wretched CD. Josh seized the CD and attempted to smash it. This was harder than he'd expected. It took several minutes, but in the end the CD gave a great crack and died. Josh broke the CD into smaller and smaller bits. Tomorrow he would present those bits to Neil.

Five

That night Josh had a strange dream. In the morning, bits of it still clung to him. He thought about it as he walked to school. He'd dreamed about something which had happened years ago, when he was no more than five or six. He had found a baby bird in the undergrowth. A tiny, grey little thing, it kept trying to fly, but it could only flutter a bit. It must have fallen out of the nest. And now it was lost and completely helpless. Josh had rushed off to get help. One of his neighbours knew all about birds. He returned with Josh at once. But when they'd got back, it had gone.

'It can't have flown off,' said Josh.

Then they found it lying quite still. Josh had been gone only a few minutes, but in that time . . . He held the bird in his hand. It was still warm. He stroked its little hanging head. He couldn't believe it was dead. He kept stroking it. Then the neighbour said, 'It's very sad, but once the baby bird fell out of the nest it never had a chance on its own, unprotected. That's the law of nature.'

And Josh had replied, 'Then it's a stupid law.'

The dream seemed to end there. Why had he remembered that again now? Was it seeing Greg lying on the road yesterday? Greg wouldn't be flattered by the comparison.

Josh thought of Greg lying in hospital. He kept thinking about that – and why Greg was there. Neil was sick, cruel. Animals were also cruel, but they couldn't help it. Human beings were different. They didn't have to follow the law of nature. They had a choice. Besides, animals didn't plot and scheme, unlike Neil carefully picking his next victim from the bottom of the school chain. And all the time Neil was totally safe.

No one would ever have traced Greg's accident back to him if Josh hadn't been passing at that very moment. If Josh had left school a few minutes earlier, as he'd planned, he'd never have seen . . . but anyway, he had seen. Maybe it was just one of those flukey things. Or maybe it was a sign that Josh had been chosen to do something, to be Greg's avenger.

The idea grew in Josh's head. He liked it. He pictured Neil, Greg's mortal enemy and now Josh's as well, waiting by the old huts for his latest delivery. He'd be shocked to see Josh turn up. And even more shocked when he discovered his precious CD in bits. It was going to be a great moment.

Josh decided the scene needed Andy as well. They were a team after all. Andy would be unwilling to join in at first, but once Josh explained the situation he was sure Andy would stand by him. It was always better having this sort of conversation face to face, which was why Josh hadn't rung Andy last night.

He grew more and more impatient, but Andy never turned up. Later, Josh discovered Andy was ill. Of all the days to be away. Andy's absence threw him at first, but he could still strike at breaktime. Yet breaktime came and went and Josh didn't do anything.

He was starting to lose his nerve. In his head he taunted himself. Then, at the end of the morning, he was summoned to see the headmaster: a mythical creature, rarely sighted except at parents' evenings. He seemed to spend most of his life on courses and, so the rumours went, at job interviews.

Josh was ushered into a quiet, air-conditioned room with blinds that were permanently drawn. He cast an envious glance at the headmaster's tall leather chair – that would look so good in H.Q. The headmaster, a large man with thick, white hair, beamed at Josh. He handed him the phone. 'Mr and Mrs Duncan want to speak to you.'

Josh could only gape at him. He'd never heard of Mr and Mrs Duncan. But after a few seconds, he realised he was talking to Greg's parents. Mrs Duncan came on the line, full of thanks.

'We're so grateful you were there,' she said.

Embarrassed, Josh tried to change the subject. 'How is Greg today?'

'Well, he didn't sleep very well, said the hospital was too noisy. But we're bringing him home this afternoon.'

'That's good.'

'And he's done nothing but talk about you. I think you're a real hero to him. I was telling the headmaster, I'm very impressed with the way you older boys look out for the younger ones. It was another older boy who found our cat. I was so impressed he'd taken so much trouble. He came right to the house, you know . . . ?'

Josh shivered while Mrs Duncan burbled on, completely unaware she was recounting a horror story. Josh could hardly stomach Mrs Duncan's thanks. Then the headmaster started oiling away to Josh about how pleased he was with the anti-bullying initiative.

As soon as he could, Josh fled to H.Q. He switched on the kettle and paced round, thinking. But he couldn't settle. He had no right to be in H.Q. He was a fraud.

He went for a walk to the shops. The weather had picked up. It was a fine, sunny day. People were shouting across the road to each other, 'Isn't it beautiful today?'

'Hope it lasts until Christmas.'

No one seemed to have a care in the world, except Josh. What was he doing here? He should be confronting Neil. Soon he would be. First he had to work out what he was going to say, find that killer phrase. But really Josh was hiding. He was running scared of Neil. No, he wasn't exactly scared of Neil – just very wary. He and Neil hardly spoke now. But that hadn't always been the case.

Once Neil had thrown all of Josh's P.E. kit into the showers. Josh had been in the first year only a few days. He scooped up all the clothes feeling angry and frightened. Then he realised Neil was watching him. And Josh immediately laughed as if he'd thought it was all a great joke. Then he had gone up to Neil and said, 'How about if I christen your P.E. kit now?' Neil just muttered something about not having his kit here. (He hardly ever brought his kit to school. Once when he'd borrowed Andy's towel, Andy threw it away immediately afterwards.) But Neil never picked on Josh again. He turned his attention to other boys in their year. One boy even changed schools because of Neil's attentions. Now all of Neil's targets were younger than him.

Something had to be done.

Then Josh spotted it. It was in the window of the Oxfam shop. An amazing coat. A Crombie. He dived into the shop. He had to try it on. Josh was tall, but very skinny. The coat should bulk him out. It transformed him. He filled the whole mirror. He was imposing. He had presence. He had to buy it.

Josh stormed back to school. He was sweltering, but he had to wear this coat. Now he had his prop or as Ally might say, he'd found his character. Wearing this coat he was a man with a mission. No one would dare stand in his way now. And he was angry again, all stoked up.

He made straight for the huts.

He recognised two guys from his year, and others from the fifth year. He hardly ever spoke to any of them. They never did anything much except get into trouble and hang about here. Were they all, to borrow Greg's phrase, Neil's deputies?

One of the fifth year boys came up to him. 'Yeah?' It was like a challenge.

Josh had a perfect right to wander round here. And yet he didn't. He was on the borders of Neil's territory. 'I've got something for Neil,' said Josh.

The boy allowed himself a look of surprise, then said, 'Brought Neil a present, have you?' The boy thought he was being funny.

Josh stared at him so hard that he walked away, disappearing into one of the huts. Typical. In class Neil always sat alone and even now he kept himself apart from his cronies. Time passed. The boy came out of the hut, nodding Josh forward.

Neil was sitting at the table, a bag of boiled sweets beside him. He stared questioningly at Josh.

'I've got something for you,' said Josh. He strode up to Neil and placed the CD on the desk.

Neil stared at the CD for a moment before picking it up. He slowly opened the case. The bits fell out on to the desk. Neil put the CD case down again, he didn't betray any surprise. But then there were whole acres of Neil's face which he never seemed to use. His reaction was oddly intimidating.

Josh dug his hands deep into his coat pockets. 'A kid got run over because of you. Now he's in hospital,' he burst out. Then he realised he'd become too emotional.

'What do you care?' said Neil softly. 'What's it to you?'

'It's a lot to me,' said Josh sounding more confident.

Neil stared at him. 'So you think you can do something about it? Go away and ask yourself why you should get involved. What's in it for you?' His voice was as low and as calm as ever.

But Josh's voice was equally controlled now. 'I'm warning you to leave Greg alone. I don't want him bullied by you – or your so-called deputies – again.'

Josh turned to go. But then he heard Neil say, 'I didn't really want the CD. I would only have given it away, luckily for you . . .' his voice dropped to a deadly undertone. 'I do hope you stay lucky.'

It was the first lesson in the afternoon and Josh was

in the same class as Neil: history with Mr Denton. It was a disaster.

At first Mr Denton had tried to be understanding with Neil. ('You've got a lot of energy, how about putting it to good use?') Then he had offered him extra lessons. ('The reason you're behaving so badly is, you don't understand what we're doing. Extra classes should help.') But Neil never turned up to these classes, while his behaviour became worse and worse.

Today, Neil and two of his cronies spent the whole time making grunting noises. Mr Denton was getting really frustrated with them. Some of the class were becoming fed up too. Mr Denton had brought in a box full of things to show the class, but he never got a chance. Finally, he totally lost his rag. He started screaming at Neil to get to the front, his chin quivering with rage. He didn't look scary though, just comical.

Neil, cool and calm, wandered up to Denton's desk with his hands in his pockets. He looked as if he didn't care about anything. Even Josh watched him with grudging admiration.

Alex whispered, 'Denton's going to crack up if he's not careful.' Neil just stood there looking Denton straight in the eye. Finally he was told to go and stand outside the headmaster's office. Not a flicker of concern crossed Neil's face. He strolled out of the classroom the undisputed victor.

Then the grunting noises started again. Only this time Mr Denton didn't seem to hear them. He dismissed the class on the bell. Then he sank back in his chair. He looked sad, hopeless. Josh had to say something. He waited until everyone clsc had gone and smiled sympathetically.

'What can I do for you?' asked Mr Denton. He was obviously still very stressed.

'Nothing, Sir. I just wanted to say – well, it's a bit harder getting them to listen if you're youngish.' He paused. Denton didn't reply. Josh pressed on. 'We had this woman here last year. She was straight out of teacher training school and people thought they could mess her about. But she said, "Anyone who says a word not relevant to this class will be punished." A minute later this boy said something silly. She made him run round the playing field three times. She became a total nightmare but . . .' Josh gave what he hoped was a significant pause.

'So that's the secret of effective teaching, is it?' said Mr Denton dryly. 'Thanks for the tip, Josh. I'd better let you get to your class, hadn't I?'

Outside Josh felt indignant and hurt. That was the last time he'd try to help a teacher

Later that same afternoon, Ally plucked up her courage and rang Josh. She was still cross with him. She still felt he'd turned his nose up at her house. But she wanted to see him again so much. Did he want to see her, though? All week she had been glaring at the phone, willing him to ring. Finally her mum said to call and invite him round for tea, then at least she'd know if he was interested or not.

'Go on, life's too short to mope about.' That was one of her mum's favourite sayings. Ally whispered it as she dialled Josh's number.

Josh answered the phone. She hadn't expected that. He sounded surprised to hear from her, but pleased. 'Don't you ever ring people?' she demanded.

'No, I leave that to my butler, Baynes. He was about to call you.'

'Well, I'd sack Baynes if I were you.'

Josh called out, 'Baynes, you're sacked.' Then he went on, 'Things have been a bit hectic, but I was going to ring you tonight, honestly.'

She just laughed and said, 'Would you or Baynes

like to come round to my house this evening for tea? My mum said it's nothing special, you'll have to take pot luck, but you'd be, as they say, very welcome. I know it's short notice, though . . .'

'I'd love to come.'

'Oh, great.' Silence for a moment.

'Well, I'd better go and look out my dinner jacket.'

'You'd better. Mum and I will be wearing our tiaras . . . See you about seven, then.'

'Accept no substitutes. I'll be there.' And he was, on the dot of seven o'clock. He wasn't wearing a dinner jacket of course, but he was wearing a smart jacket under a Crombie coat.

She offered to take his coat. 'Later,' he said. He kept his coat on until they sat down to eat. Usually they ate watching the telly, but today Ally's Mum had set the table.

Josh wasn't at all shy with her parents. He asked them about Ally's older sister, Sarah. Her parents explained that she lived in Bedford with her husband, a civil engineer, and she was expecting a baby soon. Josh seemed fascinated by every detail.

He was just so different to other boys Ally had brought back – not that there had been many. Those boys had stuttered and stumbled and the whole conversation was full of long gaps. She couldn't help feeling rather proud of Josh.

Then her dad had to rush off to work while her mum had to catch up with some marking in the study. 'Don't miss me too much, will you?' said her mum with a grin.

'Your family's all right,' said Josh. 'You're very lucky.' Ally looked up. He didn't sound as if he was just being polite. Then Josh suddenly became awkward. It was very strange. 'All right if I stretch my legs?'

'Don't even ask,' she replied.

It was a mild, light evening and her mum hated drawing the curtains too soon: she said it always made her feel closed in. Josh got up and prowled round the room. Then he looked out of the front window.

Josh stared and stared out of that window. Ally began to feel uneasy. 'Now that house opposite has got the biggest dandelions for miles around. Tourists come from all over the place.' She was smiling, but she also felt defensive again. The houses were all crammed together and although some of the gardens did look ragged and uncared for, her garden was still ablaze with red and pink roses. Her voice tightened. 'What are you looking at?'

Josh turned round. 'I'm sorry . . .' then rather too casually, 'opposite you, that's Neil's garden?'

'It certainly is. There's a plaque somewhere.'

Josh didn't look very amused.

'You said he was in your form?' she asked.

'Yes.' He frowned. Ally guessed Josh didn't like him very much. She quickly changed the subject. 'So, how's the anti-bullying counselling going?'

'I wanted to tell you about that.' And he sounded so serious, a chill ran down her back. He spoke as if it concerned her. But how could it? 'Is it all right if I tell you walking about?' asked Josh.

'Stand on your head if you like.' She spoke lightly but inside she was anxious without quite knowing why. He paced round the room, telling her about the extraordinary events of the last couple of days. When he told her about Greg rushing into the road, Ally stiffened. She had a terrible feeling he was going to tell her that he had died. She sighed with relief when she heard that he had not been seriously injured.

Suddenly Josh wasn't pacing round any more. Those large, bright eyes were staring intently at her. It was like someone shining a really strong light. He told her who was behind all this bullying.

'Neil.'

'Neil?' she repeated, then, incredulously, 'Neil across the road?'

'Does that really surprise you?' Josh's face was grim.

'Well, er . . .'

'You said you knew him well.'

All at once she was on the witness stand.

'No, not well. I mean, he's not exactly a friend or anything.' She was stumbling a bit. 'He just lives there with his mum, his dad's not around any more. I'm not sure exactly why. And his mum hardly ever leaves the house. He does all the shopping and that. And sometimes if my mum's going to the supermarket, she'll offer to get some things for them. So do I, occasionally.' Her voice fell. She felt as if she were confessing some terrible crime. 'But only now and again. I hardly know him at all, really. I definitely wouldn't call him a friend.'

This was true and yet it wasn't. Although she wasn't what you would call chummy with Neil, she did rather like him. He was always so polite to her, almost respectful. And she also felt sorry for him. It couldn't be much fun living in that house. But now Ally found herself practically denying all knowledge of him. 'So he's just an acquaintance, but what he did at your school is terrible, evil.' She hadn't meant to use that last word. But Josh seized on it.

'That's it exactly. He's evil.'

They were both looking out of the window now. The curtains opposite were drawn. Whatever secrets that house held were out of sight.

'Is Greg still in hospital?' she asked.

'No, he rang me this evening, he's at home.'

'Oh, good.'

'But he won't be at school for a few weeks yet. Tomorrow he was due to try out for the football team. That's out of the question now... I don't suppose you get any of this stuff at your school, do you?'

'We're all too busy with our embroidery, you mean.' She smiled teasingly, then said, 'When the girls at my school found out that I had an Indian father and a German mother, some of them had a field day. I got called chinky, wog, coon. Other girls would come up and ask me if my mum was a Nazi. I get called that too, sometimes. Then when I got the lead part in the school play last year, two of my so-called best friends started spreading stories about me, really nasty stories too...'

'Wow,' replied Josh. I know girls can be snidey, but I thought they were above all that other stuff.'

She burst out laughing. 'You are funny.'

Then Josh suddenly called out, 'Ally, look out.'

She nearly jumped out of her skin. Across the road the curtains were moving, and staring out was Neil. He was just there for an instant. Then the curtains closed once more. Moments later, they saw him walk up the road out of sight.

Ally gave a nervous little laugh. 'That was a bit like a pantomime, wasn't it? The villain suddenly appearing in front of the curtains.'

'Shame there was no trap-door to open under him,' replied Josh. He wasn't smiling. 'Do you think he saw us?'

'No, I don't think so. He just seemed to be staring into space.'

'I don't want him to associate you with me.' He paused. She knew what he was thinking.

She laughed again. 'Oh, I don't think he'd ever do anything to me.'

'I wonder where he's going?'

As if in reply, Ally drew the curtains. 'It's really good you want to help Greg. Not many boys would.'

Josh's eyes glittered. He gave a kind of mock swagger, 'Well, I'm not most boys.'

'You will be careful, though?' she whispered.

He gave her one of his lavish smiles then he put his arms round her. They held on to each other. She didn't ever want him to leave.

Next day the sun shone again, but this time it was shining personally on Josh. He'd never seen a more beautiful morning. He ambled to school in a happy dream. He wondered if Ally were feeling the same.

Andy was waiting for him. 'Like the coat,' he called out. 'But aren't you a bit hot?'

'This is a coat for all weathers,' said Josh, coming up to Andy.

'You're looking very pleased with yourself,' said Andy.

'Am I?' Josh couldn't keep the smile off his face today.

'You've seen Bowling Ally, haven't you?'

'Could be.'

'Well, I'm pleased for you . . . just take it steady.'

'What do you mean?'

Andy sighed. 'You always end up "marrying" your girlfriends, don't you?'

'What are you talking about?'

'Every evening you're round their house, then you get out your pipe and slippers . . .'

'Ha, ha.'

'No, it's true, mate, you get totally obsessed with your girlfriends. Happens every time.'

'Not this time,' said Josh firmly.

The bell went for registration.

They began walking into school. Then Josh saw Phil eyeballing them. This brought him back down to earth. 'While you've been away,' he said to Andy, 'there've been a few developments.'

'Go on.'

'I'd better brief you right away. Let's go to H.Q.' They began walking down the corridor.

'What's that horrible smell?' declared Andy.

'Phew, it's disgusting,' said Josh.

'It smells like a burst sewer.'

'Yeah,' began Josh. Then a terrible thought flew into his head. They walked on. The smell seemed to be getting worse. Josh really hoped it was a burst sewer, but his doubts were growing.

He opened the door to H.Q. and stopped. The smell was so overpowering it pushed them back. It was like a great wall of stink.

'What's . . . ?' began Andy. The smell seemed to take his breath away. He started coughing. 'What's in there?' he gasped at last.

'We've been hit,' said Josh, but he spoke so quietly Andy didn't hear him. Then Andy started coughing again. Josh put a handkerchief over his mouth and went inside H.Q. It was baking hot. He dragged himself across to the window, condensation poured down it. He opened the window as wide as he could.

Andy stood in the doorway. He spoke through his handkerchief. 'It smells like there's some kind of dead animal in here – and why's it so hot?'

The radiator had been turned up as high as it could go. Josh bent down to switch it off and discovered a dead fish. And another . . . Four altogether. He picked one up. The smell made him retch.

Andy was right inside now. He looked at the fish in complete amazement before he started coughing and had to go outside again.

Josh slipped the fish into a carrier bag, then he scarpered down the corridor. He wasn't sure where to dump them. Mr Denton saw him. The look of amazement on his face was almost comic. Still, it wasn't every day you discovered one of your pupils sprinting down a corridor with a bag full of dead fish.

'We've had visitors,' explained Josh. 'They left their calling card.'

Mr Denton took him round to the bins at the

back of the school. Then they both returned to H.Q. Andy had found another dead fish on top of Josh's cassettes. The tapes were in their boxes, but they were all cut up. 'So I won't be playing these any more,' muttered Josh. He looked up, and for the first time, saw a black line scrawled right across the wall. It had been done with one of those pens which wouldn't rub off.

He and Andy were given permission to tidy things up for the rest of registration. The room still reeked. They both had to keep a handkerchief over their faces. Andy's practically covered his whole face. 'We'll have to spray some aftershave round,' said Josh.

'We'll need a few gallons,' replied Andy. 'I just can't figure who'd do this. I mean, it's mad.'

'It's Neil,' said Josh.

Andy looked sceptical. 'Neil? Now I know he's a nutcase.'

'I'd swear my life on it,' interrupted Josh. 'He wants to drive us out of here.' Then he started to update Andy on what had happened. The smell made them both feel sick.

Mr Denton returned. 'This is just senseless vandalism. But I'm afraid your room's going to be out of action for a while,' he said. 'Don't worry, though, we're going to relocate you.'

'No, Sir,' said Josh firmly, 'if we abandon this room, then he's won.'

'Do you know who did this, then?' Mr Denton sounded amazed.

'I know exactly who did it,' began Josh. Andy shot him a warning glance. Josh was coming perilously close to grassing up Neil. And that was always against the rules. Josh hesitated for a moment. 'You probably know who did this too, Sir,' he said.

Mr Denton took the hint. He saw Neil at the beginning of breaktime. Neil denied everything, then asked sneeringly, 'Where's your proof?'

Of course there wasn't any.

Later, Josh saw Neil in the playground with some of his deputies and called out to him.

Neil walked over. He never swung his arms or tried to look hard. He had an odd, expressionless walk. No character in it at all. He could almost be sleep-walking. He took his time. Neil was never in a hurry.

'I saw what you did,' said Josh.

Neil didn't reply at first. He just stood there, sniffing. His deputies began to laugh. 'Why do you smell of fish?' asked Neil, at last. His deputies were killing themselves with laughter now.

'So's I don't have to smell you,' replied Josh. But he only dared say this under his breath.

Six

Usually Josh hated painting and the smell of paint. This lunchtime was different, however. It had been Pat, the caretaker's idea. Ever since Josh had moved in next door to Pat he'd made a point of befriending him. 'So's he doesn't stir up trouble for us.' Whenever they made coffee they always offered a cup to Pat and he'd become quite friendly. Today, he was amazingly helpful.

Pat brought them some green paint so that they could get rid of that black scrawl – and introduce a new smell. He also lent them some white overalls, while his wife, Marie, brought along some scented candles. Pat and Marie helped with the painting too.

Pat told them there'd been a major disturbance

last night on the other side of the school. He and his wife had gone tearing off, but they hadn't seen a thing. Now he reckoned that that was just a decoy to lure them away, 'while the other idiots got to work in here.'

Pat didn't understand why they'd picked this room. 'They could have done far more damage elsewhere,' he said. 'But it was only this place they touched.'

That's when Josh explained about Neil. He saw Andy making faces at him. But Pat and Marie weren't teachers. Telling them didn't count as grassing up someone. And they were so interested that Josh found himself telling them more and more.

'Leaving dead fish,' said Marie. 'I saw a film where someone did that.'

'Oh, it's all copied,' said Josh. 'Neil hasn't got an original thought in his head.'

'This parcel arrives in the post with a nice bow on it,' said Marie, 'and they think there's a lovely present inside, but it's full of all these dead fish.'

'Say it with fish,' quipped Josh.

They all laughed.

Then Marie said, 'Leaving dead fish, it's a kind of warning, isn't it?'

The laughter began to fade.

'Now listen, if you've got any worries about this

Neil, you let me know,' said Pat. 'Because you're doing something constructive in this school.'

'About time someone did,' said Marie.

'And it's not right that Neil gets away with all this wrong-doing,' went on Pat. 'And he does, you know. There's never any consequences. All they do is suspend him. Well, what good is that? Just a few days extra holiday for him. He's laughing up his sleeve at us, isn't he?'

Josh nodded fervently.

There was a knock on the door. 'Come in,' said Josh. To his great surprise a fifth year boy walked in. From the beginning the fifth years had shown no interest in the anti-bullying scheme and they'd been highly contemptuous of the fourth year volunteers.

'Ah, you've got a customer,' said Pat. 'Good. Well, we've just about finished here.' He put down his brush and tapped Josh on the shoulder. 'Keep on fighting. This school needs people like you, Josh – and your friend here.' He pointed at Andy, who had a slightly glazed expression on his face. Pat gave a massive sniff. 'Still smells like a trawler's been in here,' he laughed, 'but you'll get used to it, I'm sure.'

'And I'll get you some more scented candles,' said Marie.

Pat and Marie left and the fifth year stretched out a hand. 'I'm Lawrence Martins.' He was as polite as someone at a job interview.

Andy shook hands. Josh took off his overalls then shook hands too. 'I heard what happened today,' said Lawrence, a tall, serious-looking boy wearing wire glasses, 'and just came to see if there was anything I could do.'

'Oh, we'll be all right,' said Josh, 'once we've got rid of the stench.' He grinned. Lawrence smiled, then glanced round him. He looked as if he wanted to say something else.

'Sit down,' said Josh.

'Thanks,' said Lawrence. He sat down. Josh sat down too and waited. Lawrence looked up. 'Do you know about Aaron?'

Josh shook his head.

'Greg isn't the only boy Neil is . . . bullying. My little brother, Aaron, is another of his victims. At first it wasn't much.' He was speaking really quietly as if he were making a confession. 'He just had to get Neil some chocolate or sweets or a few packets of crisps. But lately . . . well, now it's practically every day. Aaron can't afford it. I've given him some money too. But it's still not enough. It's like Neil is trying to push Aaron right to the limit.' Josh nodded. 'He's been in a right state at home, had a massive row with my dad at the weekend. They think he's got in with a bad crowd. I know I should do something. I want to. But on my own . . . I've never had much of a taste for fighting.'

'I understand,' said Josh slowly.

'What you're doing is really important,' said Lawrence. 'And this revenge attack, well, it shows you've got them rattled. And if there is anything I can do . . . I've got some friends you can call on too.'

'We might just do that,' said Josh. 'And tell Aaron to come and see us. He can make an appointment or just turn up. We'll be open for business again tomorrow.'

'I'll tell Aaron that,' said Lawrence. A light seemed to have come into his eyes. He shook hands with both Josh and Andy again then left.

There was silence. Neither Josh nor Andy spoke for a moment. Andy gave a strange laugh. 'That little scene,' he said, 'was weird, surreal: the way that guy was talking to us.' He gave another laugh, 'It was like we were going to right all the school's wrongs.'

'I think we can do just that,' said Josh quietly.

'What?'

'Little kids getting terrorised won't just come here for a mug of coffee and a Wagon Wheel, they'll get some protection too.'

'Of course they will,' said Andy mockingly.

'If we don't stop Neil, no one else will.' Josh's voice was even lower. 'It's us or no one, mate.'

Andy got up. He went over to the window and took a few gulps of air. He made these exaggerated breathing noises and then turned round again. 'We're not taking on Neil,' he said firmly. 'And if you think we are – well, you'd better come and sniff some air too.'

Josh slowly got to his feet. 'Oh, come on, Andy.'

Andy shook his head firmly.

'Look, we're not letting Neil get away with what he did to Greg – or to my room.'

'Your room?' exclaimed Andy. 'Well, I'm sorry, but I didn't see a name plate on the door saying exclusive property of Josh. For some reason, I thought I was in this too.'

'Of course you are,' said Josh. 'I didn't mean to say that. I wasn't thinking straight. What happened in here has been a bit of a shock.'

'At least you were prepared for something. It's been a double shock for me. I mean, two days ago we were going to stay right out of anything to do with Neil. Then behind my back . . .'

'It wasn't behind your back.'

'Of course it was.'

Their voices rose. 'Look, you were away and things happened,' said Josh. 'I had to do something.'

'You should have kept me briefed.'

'I was going to.'

Andy made a scoffing noise, then turned away and began breathing out of the window again. He inhaled as if he really needed the air.

Josh hesitated. His throat felt very tight. 'Okay, Andy, I'm committed to this, but you're not. So you can stay right out of it. It's not your fight.'

Andy whirled round. 'You get me so mad sometimes.'

'Now what have I said?'

'What do you mean "it's not my fight"?' Andy snapped. 'All I wanted was to be consulted, but you couldn't do that, could you? You've got an ego the size of Kent.' He glared at Josh.

Josh gave an apologetic smile. 'Actually, my ego's much bigger than Kent.' Andy couldn't help smiling. Then he sighed loudly. Josh moved towards him. 'I need you in this with me, mate.'

'No you don't.'

'Stop arguing. I do.'

Andy began to pace about. 'The way you stood up for Greg earlier was mad, but in a warped kind of way I was proud of you.'

Josh bowed.

'But we're not taking on some little first year who makes fun of geezers with ginger hair.'

'I know.'

Andy sighed again. 'So let me get this straight, it's you and me against Neil and all his gang.'

'There'll be others helping us.'

'Like who?'

'That fifth year said he'd help.'

'Didn't he also say he hadn't much of a taste for fighting? Neither, by the way, have you – or me.' He paused expectantly.

Josh sat down again. 'We're not going to fight them, Andy,' he said in a far-off voice. 'Nothing so tacky. We're going to defeat them with our superior brain power.'

'Are you serious?'

'Totally. Andy, we can change this school if we want.'

'What are you on today? Can I have some?'

Josh grinned. 'You're right about one thing, though, we need some more recruits . . . So, who would you like?'

'What?'

'Name someone you'd like on our team.'

'Just like that.'

'Yeah, go on.'

'Well, we need someone with a bit of muscle, like Kane.'

'Okay. I'll get Kane to join us.'

Andy smiled disbelievingly. 'He won't be interested.'

'Yes he will,' said Josh. 'Not right away, I'll grant you. But there's a way to everyone.'

Josh saw Kane standing by the lockers. There was no mistaking him. A massive guy. He had the biggest arm muscles Josh had ever seen. Kane didn't look for hassle. He didn't have anything to prove. But when he turned, you knew about it. Josh had seen him pick people up and throw them against the wall.

Josh grinned at him. 'I was talking about you last night.'

Kane started. 'Who to?'

'Who do you think? My sister.'

Kane couldn't believe his ears. For weeks he'd been sending notes and little gifts to Lucy without any response at all. Now Josh had all Kane's attention.

'What did she say?'

'Oh, she's interested in you all right,' said Josh. 'But she's a bit scared of you, too.'

'Scared?'

'Well, you're a pretty fearsome guy.' Kane took this as a compliment. 'But like I say, she's been mentioning you a lot. I might be able to talk her round.' Kane looked surprised. He and Josh weren't especially good friends. 'I was just wondering,' went on Josh, 'if I could ask you a little favour in return?'

'Now, Lucy, I'm not putting you under any pressure,' said Josh.

She laughed mockingly. They were in her bed-room. She was lying on her bed. Josh was sitting on the chair by her dressing table. 'It's just, one date with Kane tomorrow could save a boy from being bullied. It's up to you.'

She paused. 'But Kane's so awful. He'll slobber over me all evening.'

'Lucy, he'll do whatever you tell him.'

She thought for a moment. 'I can't talk to him.'

'You won't have to,' said Josh.

'What?'

'Listen to me. You'll meet at the pictures, right, he'll buy you popcorn.'

'I hate popcorn.'

'A choc ice, then. After which you go and see a film, of your choice, of course.'

'And he keeps his hands to himself.'

'Absolutely. Lucy, you're like a goddess to him.' She made sick noises. 'And then you say goodbye, hop into a taxi paid for by me, and come home.' He paused. 'You'd be doing me a big favour.'

She sighed loudly.

'Thanks,' said Josh. He got up. 'Done your homework, then?'

'Not yet.'

'Well, see you do it. You're clever and you should pass every exam there is.'

'Yes, Daddy.'

'Just don't ever call me step-dad.'

'Don't worry, I'd never ever call you that,' said Lucy. 'No matter what you did. Never,' she added emphatically.

They grinned at each other.

'I knew you wouldn't let me down,' said Josh softly.

*

'And what would you do if it was your brother lying in that hospital?' said Josh.

'I'd laugh,' said Andy.

'What?' Josh lifted his eyes up from his speech. Both he and Andy were in H.Q. before school started.

'I'm sorry, but that's what they'll say,' said Andy. 'It's far too corny.'

'Okay, all right,' said Josh, putting his pen through those lines. He'd invited six boys, including Kane, to a private meeting after school tomorrow, to explain to them the idea of the Protectors. Josh had sent out proper cards and put 'coffee will be served' at the bottom. But he was having great trouble with his speech. 'Let me try the next bit on you, Andy.'

Ally was about to race out of the door for her rehearsal. The phone rang. Her mum picked it up, and Ally mouthed, 'I've gone.'

But then she heard her mum say, 'Hello, Josh, I'll see if I can catch her.' She looked questioningly at Ally.

Ally nodded and took the phone. She was puzzled, she'd spoken to Josh about two hours ago and he knew she had a rehearsal tonight.

'Ally, have you got two minutes?'

'Just about.'

'Well, I'm ringing you from the school.'

'What are you doing there?'

'I can think better in H.Q. and Pat's let me use his phone. Look, I've got to make this speech tomorrow.'

'I know.'

'Yeah, well I've made a few last minute changes and I'd just like you to hear them. Have you got time?'

She hadn't at all.

He said, 'This speech has got to be really good tomorrow and I don't think it is yet. In fact, I know it isn't.'

She had never heard him sound so nervous, so vulnerable. She sat down on the chair by the phone. 'Go on, then,' she said.

'And why is Neil doing this? I'll tell you exactly,' said Josh. 'Just for the pleasure of seeing these boys being pushed further and further until they crack, until he destroys them. Some of them are very near to breaking point now.'

Josh let that bit sink in, while Andy gazed round at the audience squashed into H.Q. Lawrence Martins was there with three other fifth years. So was Kane with one of his mates, Alex. Now Alex could look after himself, but Kane was the prize.

At the beginning of Josh's speech there'd been little bursts of conversation between Kane and Alex. Josh was well-known and fairly well-liked as the quick-witted clown of the class, but he wasn't viewed as a leader. There was a feeling amongst those two that maybe Josh was getting above himself. But then Josh told Greg's story, he also told it as a story against himself. He kept repeating how he and Andy had let Greg down. The murmurs began to fade. 'So bullying is everywhere in this school. It's in the air we breathe. It's like a great thick fog covering everything.'

Andy hadn't heard that part before. That must be one of the bits he'd added with Ally last night. He had discussed it with her for hours, apparently. Andy thought Josh was going over the top now. But the audience still seemed to be with him.

'You may say,' continued Josh, 'what does it matter? Little kids are persecuted, so what, it's just another part of the rotten history of this school. Why should we do anything? We'll pass by, keep our heads down, hope it will never be us – or our little brothers.' Josh gave a quick glance at Lawrence Martins. 'So we let an evil maggot like Neil run the school.'

Prefects.' Josh raised his eyes to heaven at the
idea. 'Prefects are two-a-penny. We're a
ally-selected elite group.'

Doing what?' asked Alex.

We're like a peace-keeping force,' said Josh,
king life as difficult as possible for Neil and his
of mutants. We'll be a constant presence behind
ny lines until he changes his ways. And he will.'

paused. 'We're going to confront all the bullying
ee, and always protect the weak. That's why we're
d the Protectors.' There were smiles at the name
he idea was starting to take hold too.

Now, I'm inviting you to join the Protectors, but
each be on two weeks' probation. After two
s you will be asked to join the Protectors and
the full members' kit – or asked to leave.'

nd it's you who decides this?' asked Alex.

le and Andy, yes.'

ere was some stirring at this. Josh pressed on.

other thing: all the Protectors have to wear a
black tie when they're on duty.'

s is what Andy had argued with Josh about
ay. Andy thought the tie was pushing things
ch. This risked losing everyone's support.

y have we got to wear a tie?' asked Lawrence.

'He doesn't run the school,' said

'Yes he does,' said Lawrence Mar
running scared of him.'

'I'm not,' said Kane firmly.

'Let's say Neil thinks he runs th
Josh. 'I think it's time we stopped hi
murmurs of agreement.

'Here's our plan of action,' said J
out some photocopied sheets which
earlier that day. There was a map of
even a little compass in the corner.
impressed by this handout. It made the
seem more businesslike, somehow. 'No
out areas where the enemy are stror
for instance, are a key target. What v
behind the enemy lines and reclaim

'Fight them, you mean?' said A

'No,' said Josh firmly. 'Let me s[
carefully. Look round you at our
Andy's. This hasn't just happened.
We want to get you a room too, an
But we've got to play by certain r
start fighting we'll be closed dow
up for everyone.'

'So we're just like prefects?'

'It's essential we stand out and people know who the Protectors are,' said Josh. 'It's also important we're smart.'

'Why?' demanded Kane.

'Because Neil and his deadheads never look smart,' said Josh.

'Well, I think that's pathetic,' said Alex.

There were ripples of agreement.

'Have we got to pay for the tie?' asked Lawrence.

'I've been given an allowance to pay for the damage to this room,' replied Josh, 'but I can use the money to help towards your uniform, if you wish.'

'We'll look so stupid,' said Alex.

'Anyone not wanting to do this,' said Josh, 'is perfectly free to leave now.' He spoke calmly but little beads of sweat were forming on his forehead.

Andy came to his aid. 'I don't like ties much, but we need to wear them to get proper respect . . . you only have to wear them when you're on duty.'

'So if we're a Protector we have to wear a tie?' persisted Kane.

'Yes,' said Josh. 'It's compulsory.'

Kane shifted in his chair. The fifth years exchanged glances.

Finally, Kane said, 'So where do we get these ties from, then?'

Josh shot Andy a grin. 'Leave that to me.'

Seven

'Whose funeral are you going to?'

'Yours, if you don't shut up.' Alex raised his fist. Josh gave a warning cry. The boy scarpered.

'If one more person says that,' muttered Alex.

'Don't get aggressive,' said Josh. 'People are bound to be curious. We're something new.'

It was Monday lunchtime. The Protectors were on duty for the first time. In addition to the tie, Josh was wearing a black jacket underneath his Crombie coat. He had positioned the Protectors all round the school and Andy was keeping an eye on H.Q. Josh and Alex were on their way to the huts – their key target. Kane was supposed to be joining them, although there was no sign of him at that moment.

As they approached the huts, the air became foggy with cigarette smoke. Behind the huts, boys were whispering and laughing and music blared out. Three of Neil's gang stood at the bottom step of one of the huts. They looked like bouncers barring entry to a nightclub. One of them was Phil. The other two were fifth years. At Hallowe'en, thought Josh, all three of them could get by without masks.

'Who's died?' one of them called out. Josh and Alex ignored this. They stood together like a two-man picket line.

'What are you wearing those ties for?' asked Phil.

'Good question,' murmured Alex.

'Because we're the Protectors,' said Josh. 'That's why.'

Phil and the other two boys exchanged sniggers. 'So what are you doing here?' asked Phil.

'You'll see,' said Josh.

Phil didn't ask any more questions. Instead, he disappeared inside the hut.

'Gone to tell Neil,' said Josh. 'We're getting to them already,' he added hopefully.

More boys emerged from behind the huts. They stood staring at Josh and Alex.

'Where's Kane got to?' muttered Alex. He and

Josh shifted uncomfortably. None of Neil's boys was particularly big, bright or good at sports. They were all congealed together at the bottom of the school. Did that account for the eerie blankness of their faces? They weren't Neil's gang. They were his clones. A pack of zombies. They didn't care about anything. Maybe that was why they were so dangerous.

Phil came out of the hut. He whispered something and at once they all broke into loud laughter, but without humour.

'We're making a right show of ourselves here,' said Alex. He turned towards the football match on the back field. 'That's where we should be, not on this human rubbish tip.'

Josh didn't want to be here either. Then to his great relief, he saw Kane thumping towards them. Neil's gang immediately faded away. Kane was late, but Josh didn't say a word. Kane pulled at his black tie. He'd obviously just lobbed it on over his blue and white lumberjack shirt, unlike Josh who'd arranged his tie with style.

'I hate having something round my neck,' said Kane.

'I know,' said Alex. 'You feel like you're being

choked, don't you?' The knot in his tie was the size of a plum.

'You'll get used to it,' said Josh quickly. 'Anyway, girls go for guys in ties, it's a scientific fact.'

'In case it has escaped your notice,' said Alex, 'there aren't any girls here.'

'The word will get round,' said Josh. 'You'll see.'

'So what's been happening?' asked Kane.

'Apart from us making total prats of ourselves? Absolutely nothing,' replied Alex.

'Give it time,' said Josh.

More time crawled past, then something did happen. A small, chubby boy appeared. Josh noticed how Phil and his cronies seemed to come alive, like hunters who'd just spotted their prey. Behind the hut the music was switched off.

'He's got to be making a delivery,' said Josh. 'Here's where we step in.' He strode over to the boy. 'Excuse me, but what are you doing here?'

The boy kept his head down. He acted as if he hadn't heard the question. Then Alex and Kane began circling round him too. The boy very slowly looked up.

'What are you doing here?' repeated Josh.

'Mind your own business,' cried the boy shrilly.

'We've made it our business,' said Alex.

'You're here to see Neil, aren't you?' said Kane. The boy shrank back from his gaze. 'I might be.'

'Well, you're not going to see Neil,' said Kane.

'Why?' gasped the boy.

'Wayne, be careful,' called Phil suddenly. The boy turned to him.

He gulped. Then he looked up at Kane again. 'What are you, some other gang?'

'No, we're not. We're the Protectors.' Josh's tone softened. 'Now listen, Wayne, we know you're here to make a delivery to Neil. But what we're saying is, you needn't do it. You can turn round and go back. We'll help you now.'

'Wayne, you're late for your appointment,' called Phil.

Wayne was beginning to panic. 'Please let me pass,' he begged.

'No one's keeping you here,' said Josh wearily.

The boy looked up at them again, then darted off towards the hut. A moment later he and Phil had disappeared inside.

'Well, we can't protect a guy who doesn't want to be protected, can we?' said Alex.

Kane began undoing his tie. 'I'm sorry, but this

thing's just too tight round my neck.'

Josh only smiled grimly.

The boy wasn't in the hut very long. He came out, clearly distressed. Josh went up to him. 'What's happened, Wayne?'

He suddenly turned on Josh. 'You've ruined everything.'

'What are you talking about?' Alex and Kane were hovering beside him.

'Neil said I shouldn't have spoken to you. I should have just ignored you and come straight to him. Now I've failed the test.'

'What test?' asked Josh.

'Neil wanted a lighter. He promised he'd leave me alone if I got him one, but now, because I delayed, he won't accept it. I've got to keep it.' He dug the lighter out of his pocket and waved it accusingly at them. 'It's no use to me and if I take it home my mum'll go mad. So now I'm still in Neil's debt . . . all because of you.'

'Wayne, listen to me, you're not in Neil's debt,' said Josh.

'You don't know what you're talking about.'

'Just answer me this, you nicked that lighter, didn't you?'

'No,' he gasped.

'Are you sure?' asked Josh.

'Leave me alone,' screamed Wayne, flinging the lighter down on the grass and running away. Josh stared after him. Behind him came loud, mocking laughter.

'What are we doing trying to help some ignorant little tyke like that?' said Alex.

'He was scared,' interrupted Josh.

'He'd better not speak to me like that,' said Alex. 'Little guy like that mouthing off to fourth years. And listen to those hyenas, they think we're just a big joke.'

Kane murmured in agreement.

Josh had been deeply disappointed too, but he couldn't let them see that. Instead, he bent down and picked up the lighter. 'It's quite heavy and chunky, nice lighter all right. I bet Neil's gutted to lose this, really.'

'I'm glad you think so,' replied Alex. 'Personally, I think we're all just wasting our time.'

It wasn't going well.

The Protectors were wandering about the school like guests at a party who had mistakenly arrived in fancy dress. They looked self-conscious and awkward.

Neil didn't seem at all bothered by them taking up residence on his turf. If anything, it seemed to add to his pleasure, watching the little first years scurry past the Protectors, anxious not to incur his wrath.

Josh doubted if Alex and Kane would stay members much longer. And even Andy had an I-told-you-it-wouldn't-work look on his face. It was very disheartening. He'd hardly seen Ally these past few days. He hadn't been at home much either. Not that he minded. His home seemed to have less and less to do with him. He couldn't change anything there. And he didn't want to risk losing control again with his step-dad.

But here in H.Q., he knew he could achieve things, make a difference, yet no one really seemed to share his vision. Not even Mr Denton.

One day he commented to Josh, 'I don't see why you need to march round the school in black ties.'

'It's so people will know who we are,' said Josh quietly.

'But surely they know who you are anyway?' said Mr Denton.

'The ties are there to make us look smart, efficient.' Josh stared into his coffee cup. He felt embarrassed saying that as Mr Denton never wore a tie. But a smile was forming at the corners of the teacher's mouth.

'You realise, Josh, if ties were compulsory I'd probably be telling you off now for not wearing one. This school does not need a band of self-appointed vigilantes stirring up more trouble.'

Actually, Josh did think of the Protectors as a bit like vigilantes, if non-violent ones. They were outlaws, operating outside the law, but always on the side of the weak and the downtrodden. Still, he nodded in agreement with Mr Denton.

'And if there's any fighting at all . . .'

'There won't be, Sir. It's just a natural extension of our counselling, really. Only we're out and about trying to stop the bullying before it happens. We'll just be out patrolling, helping anyone who comes to us. We'll be the eyes and ears of the school.'

'But you're carrying on the counselling as well?'

'Oh, yes, of course.'

'All right. Now, what is it you call yourselves? The Protectors?'

A smile twitched at his mouth again. He was humouring Josh. He didn't believe for a moment that the Protectors could work. But even if no one had faith in it, Josh would not give up. He could not. He'd show them all.

Next morning, before school started, Josh went to see Pat, the caretaker. Pat was Josh's only real ally. He thought the Protectors was an absolutely marvellous scheme. He even liked the black ties and said Josh looked better dressed than most of the teachers now. Josh explained to him about his idea and by lunchtime Pat had put locks on both the hut doors so Neil wouldn't be able to lord it over everyone from the huts any more. But the locks were quickly and expertly vandalised. By lunchtime, Neil was back inside.

Next day, Pat put giant padlocks on the two doors. They climbed in through the windows. Now Pat's blood was up. He put locks on all the windows too, and declared, 'I've been round every corner of those huts, not even a spider could break in there now.'

Josh wanted to see Neil locked out of his domain. He wanted to gloat a bit but instead, Aaron, Lawrence's brother turned up unexpectedly at H.Q. He was the first person officially to ask the Protectors for help.

Lawrence had tried to get Aaron to see Josh and Andy before, but he'd refused. Lawrence was highly embarrassed but Josh said, 'Leave it, he'll turn up in his own time.' Josh had sounded more confident than he felt. He had been getting quite desperate. Here they were, the Protectors, protecting absolutely no one.

So Aaron's appearance was a bit of a milestone.

Aaron told them how Neil was upping the pressure on him and while the Protectors continued he wanted sweets and chocolate every day, not just once a week.

Neil had hoped to turn Aaron against the Protectors, but he'd pushed too hard. Instead, Aaron talked and talked. He told them how Neil's gang also operated along the lunch queues, regularly 'borrowing' money from the first and second years, without ever returning it, of course.

'We'll need to put someone on there at lunchtime,' said Andy to Josh. Then he turned to Aaron, 'If ever you're worried or if Neil bothers you, come straight to us, understand? We're open every lunchtime.'

For once, Andy was doing all the talking. Josh sat back, chuffed to bits that Andy had suddenly realised what the Protectors could be. 'And don't worry, we'll be keeping a discrete eye on you, too,' said Andy.

A knock on the door, two sharp raps which meant it was one of the Protectors. 'Sorry to interrupt,' said

Lawrence, 'but Kane said can you both come right now?'

'What's up?' asked Josh.

'Don't worry, it's just something Kane thinks you should both see. Will you follow me?'

'Where are we going?' asked Andy.

'I'm not allowed to tell you. Kane wanted it to be a surprise.'

Josh stared at Lawrence intrigued. He seemed incredibly happy about something. Lawrence turned to his brother, 'I think this is something you should see, too.'

They made their way over to the back field. The Protectors were still an object of curiosity, but the jokes had stopped. When they were on patrol, little groups of younger boys hovered round them now.

The huts loomed ahead.

'Notice anything?' asked Lawrence, grinning all over his face.

Josh's hunch proved correct. 'The vermin have all gone,' he said, his face one big smile. 'And they never even left us a forwarding address.' Alex and Kane came running over. Then they all laughed and cheered and waved their fists victoriously.

'Just smell that fresh, unpolluted air,' said Josh. 'Did you ever smell anything like that?'

'What made them go?' asked Lawrence.

'We did . . . and Pat,' cried Alex, slamming his fist into the air again.

'I don't think Neil could stand the loss of face,' said Andy slowly. 'We've driven him out of his hut. He can't pose about in there any more. He'll have to find somewhere else now.'

'Where do you think he's gone?' asked Lawrence.

'Wherever it is, we'll find him,' said Josh firmly. 'Anyway, this is our first major victory. We've reclaimed the huts.'

'Maybe we should put a flag up,' said Aaron. Everyone laughed good-humouredly.

'You are still the Protectors, then?' said a voice behind them. It was Wayne, the boy who, last week, had thrown a lighter at Josh. His tone wasn't any more friendly.

'That's right. We're the Protectors,' said Josh.

'Well, I need your help,' he snapped.

'Just tell us one thing first, squirt,' said Alex, leaning down so that his face was almost touching Wayne's. 'You did steal that lighter, didn't you?'

'No, no,' squealed Wayne.

'Alex,' said Josh warningly. Alex reluctantly backed off.

Josh was careful not to crowd the boy and he spoke as if he were addressing a nervous puppy. 'Now, in your own time, tell us how we can help you.'

The boy took a deep breath. 'They've been on at me again, said they want daily deliveries from me for as long as the Protectors are operating in the school . . . Well, I can't do that.'

So they were trying the same tactic on Wayne as they had on Aaron. And again it seemed to be backfiring.

'I'm glad you came to us, Wayne,' said Josh. 'May I just ask when Neil told you this?'

'Just now.'

'And where was he?' asked Andy.

'By the bike racks. They were all there.'

'I thought he might go there,' said Alex.

'We knew they'd have to migrate somewhere,' murmured Josh. 'But we'll drive him out of there, too. Now, Wayne, listen to me, just ignore everything Neil said to you. We're going to look after you now, all right?'

'Thanks,' said Wayne very quietly. Then he burst out, 'I didn't steal that lighter, you know.'

'We believe you,' said Josh.

'We've got this jar where my mum keeps change. I took some money out of there, but it wasn't enough.' His shoulders began to shake and he could only whisper, 'So I took five pounds out of my mum's purse. I only did it the once and I didn't want to, but I had no choice.'

Josh put a hand on Wayne's shoulder. 'You've had some bad days, Wayne, but they're all over. You're in the Protectors' hands now. Lawrence, will you take Aaron and Wayne back to H.Q. and make them a coffee? Andy and I will join you there very soon.'

After they'd set off, Josh turned to the other Protectors. 'We've won the first battle, but not the war, yet. Our first priority is to keep those two guys safe – and Greg too, when he comes back next week. We must also make sure this area remains under our "command".'

'These next days are going to be vital,' said Andy.

'And we can't afford to be half-hearted,' said Kane. 'I'm happy to volunteer for extra duties.'

Josh stared at Kane in surprise. Lucy wasn't keen to go on any future dates with Kane. Josh had assumed he would start to lose interest in the group.

'I think we're going to need some more recruits,' went on Kane.

'We'll get them,' said Josh. 'Only they've got to be high-calibre people.'

'So, are we still on probation?' asked Alex.

'You'll find out tomorrow,' said Josh, 'when I shall be inviting the successful applicants to sign up as full-scale Protectors.'

*

PROTECTOR MEMBERSHIP CARD

I PROMISE THAT ....

I will protect all the pupils at my school.

I will not use violence unless it is absolutely necessary.

I will not bring the Protectors into disrepute.

I will be fair and, without any prejudice, help people.

I must always be correctly dressed when undertaking Protectors' Business.

Signed: ....

Authorised by: ....

LOYALTY IS EVERYTHING

*

Eight

Greg stood outside Smedleys. He couldn't believe it. The shop had definitely shrunk. Or maybe it just grew at night, in nightmares. He never thought he'd make this journey again. But every evening Josh had rung him. And Josh was like his coach, urging him forward, assuring him he had nothing to fear now as the Protectors would always look after him. He also told Greg that if he didn't come back, this meant the bullies had won. And bullies must never be allowed to win.

Greg walked slowly. His right leg was strapped up and he still got these twinges of sharp pain. He stopped suddenly. He had a horrible feeling he was being followed. He looked round sharply. He couldn't see anyone. Then he heard someone call his name.

Greg wasn't sure what to do. He felt weak and ill again. A boy ran towards him. His chest was as big as a wardrobe. Greg shrank back. The boy stretched out a hand. 'You're Greg, aren't you?'

He nodded cautiously.

'Josh said you'd be carrying a book under your arm, but you're earlier than I was expecting.'

'Who are you?' gasped Greg.

'I'm Kane, just look on me as your personal bodyguard. Josh said to escort you to school. He thought you might be feeling a bit nervous. But you look all right to me. Come on, then.'

Greg and his 'bodyguard' walked into school together. Greg had to half-run to keep up. Josh was waiting by the gate. He was wearing a dark suit, a white shirt and a thin, black tie. Greg thought he looked older and dead smart.

'Hey, welcome back. How are you feeling?'

'Much better, thanks.'

'Brilliant, brilliant.' Josh pumped his hand. 'You'll see some changes to this school.'

Kane laughed. 'He won't recognise the place. Anyway, I'm off to do a quick inspection of the huts.'

'The huts belong to us now,' said Josh. 'But I told you about that, didn't I?'

Greg nodded solemnly.

'See you both later,' said Kane, 'and remember, call on me any time, Greg.' He patted Greg on the back. He was about to go when Josh called him. He turned round. Josh was grinning and pointing at his neck. 'Don't worry, it's in my pocket. I'll put it on as soon as I'm officially on duty. I promise, Sir,' added Kane, mock-humbly.

'Good man,' said Josh. He stared after him. 'One of our best Protectors, totally committed to the cause.'

'The cause?' repeated Greg.

'We're cleaning up the school, Greg. What happened to you will never happen again – to anyone. And you're the one who started it all.' He grinned. 'You and that case.'

Greg smiled too.

'Anyway, I'd better go. I'm expecting a delivery. But how about coming to see me at H.Q. at the beginning of lunch?'

'Yes,' said Greg.

And Greg was there, on the dot of twelve-fifteen. He knocked, opened the door, then gaped in amazement. Josh was reclining in a black leather armchair. 'How long have you had that?'

Josh looked at his watch. 'Three and a quarter hours, arrived this morning.'

'It's excellent.'

'I just knew I had to have a more imposing chair. I've been searching for ages for something . . . sit down.'

'And you've painted the walls.'

'We had some visitors so we had to clean up pretty quickly. But I'm going to paint the walls again soon. Have no fear. No, I've got big plans for this place – and the school. What do you think of the Protectors?'

'Everyone's talking about them.'

'And Neil hasn't bothered you?'

'I haven't seen him.'

'Yeah, he seems to be lying low.'

Andy came in, also wearing a suit and white shirt, as well as a black tie. 'Greg, I heard you were back. How are you feeling?'

'Just fine,' said Greg.

'Josh told you about the football team, then?'

'No,' began Greg.

'We hadn't got round to that, yet. Give us a chance.' He leaned forward. 'I've been to see the P.E. teacher, Mr Denton came too, and there's a place on the team for you when you're fit.'

'What?' cried Greg.

'He'll want to tell you himself so look surprised when he does, but it's fixed.'

'Brilliant.' Greg was genuinely overcome. 'I wanted to be in the team so much, so when I had my accident I thought it was all over. Thank you, Josh, thank you.'

Josh looked pleased.

'How many other pupils are you protecting?' asked Greg.

'There are seven on the books at the moment, including you. But the latest intelligence is that there are other pupils still to come to us. Our door is always open to them.'

'Then there are those boys who complain they're being pestered for money in the dinner queue, at the bike racks, places like that,' said Andy. 'We want to protect them too.'

'I can't believe you're going to all this trouble,' said Greg. 'If ever I can do anything for you. I mean, I know I can't do much . . .'

'It's good to know we can come to you,' said Josh.

There was a knock on the door. 'I think that's our first interviewee,' said Andy.

'We've got six more applicants to be Protectors, including two more fifth years,' said Josh.

'And we'll need them,' said Andy.

'I'd better go then, but thanks for everything.' Greg got up, glowing with excitement and gratitude.

'No problem,' said Josh. 'And remember, call on us anytime.'

'I will.' Greg bounded down the corridor nearly colliding with Mike, the boy who'd once warned him against crossing Neil.

'Hello,' said Mike. 'Hear you had a bit of an accident.'

'Yes, but I'm better now.'

'Seen Neil yet?'

'No, and I'm not going to either,' said Greg firmly.

'I've just seen him,' said Mike.

'Have you?'

'He's not happy.'

'Isn't he?' Greg's confidence was starting to ebb away.

'These Protectors have really stirred him up. He's demanding I get him all these things. I don't think he even wants half of them.'

'It's just the power he likes,' said Greg.

'That's right,' agreed Mike. 'But what can you

do? I'd never want to cross him. I've heard what he does to people who cross him.'

'But we've got the Protectors now. Neil can't touch you – or me – any more.'

Mike looked doubtful. 'Neil's got a way of striking when you least expect it.'

'Not any more.' Greg pointed at a boy in a black tie standing by the lunch queue. 'Wherever Neil operates, a Protector will be there blocking him. They're getting some more Protectors today, as well.'

'So the Protectors really can stop Neil? I needn't do what Neil says?'

'Right, why don't you go and see Josh now. He's interviewing, but I'm sure he'll see you.'

'You reckon?'

'Yes, yes. Tell Josh it's an emergency, tell him I sent you.'

'I might just do that.'

'Go on, do it now,' urged Greg, copying the way Josh spoke to him on the phone. It seemed to be working with Mike too.

Greg found out later that Mike had gone to H.Q. and was now officially 'protected'. Greg was delighted. He looked out for Mike, but it was two days before he saw him again. When he did, Greg stared at him in horror: he was sporting a massive black eye, his nose was bruised too. And his right hand was bandaged. He looked as if he could hardly stand up.

Before Greg could say anything, Mike declared, 'I just walked into a door, all right.' He sounded angry and very defensive. Yet he winced as he spoke. His usual oily confidence had gone completely. He hobbled away. By breaktime, the deputy headmistress had driven him home. He'd keeled over in the middle of a lesson.

Rumours about Mike flew round the school. The story was that he'd been set upon by Neil and his gang the night before last. He'd been walking his dog when these figures appeared out of nowhere.

There was another rumour too.

This was just the first strike.

More were to follow.

Nine

As soon as she got back from school, Ally rang Josh. She had never known him to sound so defeated. When she heard who had been beaten up, the name rang a bell. She was sure she knew him vaguely.

'And of course, all the other boys who came to us are bricking it now, wondering who'll be next,' said Josh. 'None of them has said anything, but I know what they're thinking. I can see it in their eyes. I've let them down.'

'No you haven't. You've rescued them. You've given them hope.'

'False hope. I should have realised Neil would do something. He deliberately lulled us into a false sense of security then, out of the blue, he struck.

He's a much cleverer operator than I gave him credit for.'

Last night Josh had been so different. He'd invited her round to 'his place'. She'd assumed he meant his house. Instead, he took her to the school and his H.Q. He showed her round, insisted she try out the leather chair and explained how he wanted to get a dark green desk lamp next, as 'lighting can just make or break a room'. Then he told her that he was here most nights now.

She was astounded. 'But what do you do here?'

'Well, once I've sorted out all my rotas and general paper work to do with the Protectors, I do homework, listen to my music, laugh at my own jokes . . . think about you.'

Later, Pat arrived with a plateful of cheese and ham sandwiches for them both and declared, 'Josh is as snug as a badger in his sett here.'

'Don't you just love the atmosphere?' Josh said. Ally would never have thought of a room in an empty school at night as having any atmosphere at all. Yet, it was different here. It was like Josh's bedroom. His kingdom. Now she knew why he hadn't taken her to his house. He only lodged there. He lived here!

That night at H.Q. he spoke for ages about Neil. 'Every time Neil tries to do something, we'll be there too, blocking him all the way.' Victory had seemed to be within his grasp. It was awful the way everything was crumbling away now.

After she'd put the phone down, Ally had to get ready for her rehearsal. She walked quickly to the church hall, her mind still full of what Josh had said. Suddenly she couldn't believe what she'd just seen. She turned back and took a second look. And a third. It didn't make any sense. Then, all at once, it did. She dived into a phone box. She had to tell Josh immediately. She knew the number of his home off by heart. Let him be in.

'You've just missed him,' said his mum. 'I'm not sure where he's gone to. These days he never tells me anything.'

Ally was certain he'd be at his H.Q. But going there would make her late for her rehearsal.

She hesitated for just a second.

Ally saw Pat in the school entrance.

'I don't suppose Josh is around?'

'Of course he is. I told him he'll be bringing his sleeping bag here soon. Still, we don't mind. There

143

aren't many boys we'd let roam round here. But he's a good lad, isn't he?' He gave Ally a look. Suddenly he was acting like a proud parent. He escorted Ally down the corridor. Then he knocked and opened the door.

Josh was sitting in his leather chair shuffling his papers just like they do at the end of *News at Ten*. He looked so desperately sad, her heart went out to him. Pat left as noiselessly as any butler. Josh got up to greet her. 'This is a surprise.'

'I can't stop, but there's something I have to tell you.'

Josh squeezed her arm. 'What's wrong?'

'Nothing's wrong, exactly. That boy who got attacked, he was called Mike Archer, wasn't he?'

'Yes.'

'Right, well, Mike Archer lives quite near me. I only know him vaguely, but that's why his name rang a bell. I pass his house most days and tonight I saw him in his front garden kicking a ball around. There's nothing wrong with him. There's not a mark on his face. I mean, I took a second look. I couldn't believe it.'

'And it really was Mike Archer?' He said this very slowly.

'Yes, because I know him. And he was perfectly well, no bandages . . . nothing.'

He stared at her. Then a smile crept across his face. He wiped his brow with his arm, while his smile just grew and grew. Now he was staring right at her.

'What?' she cried at last.

'I was just thinking,' said Josh.

'Yes?'

'I was thinking that what you did for me tonight is something I shall remember for the rest of my life. You really came through for me,' his voice caught a little. Then he was hugging her and whispering, 'Thank you, thank you,' into her ear. She snuggled closer to him until finally, he gently let go of her and started pacing round the room.

'I saw that weasel, Mike, today, you know. I was looking out of the window and my first thought was, he's limping a bit too much, because people always overdo it when they're pretending to be ill, don't they? If only I'd acted on that suspicion . . . still, that little stunt must mean they're running scared of the Protectors. That's why they've tried to put the frighteners on us.'

He rattled on until she said suddenly, 'I'm sorry, I've got to go, if I'm not at this rehearsal . . .'

'Of course. Just wait one second.' She heard him talking to Pat, then he rushed back. 'A taxi has been called in your honour and will await your regal posterior in precisely two minutes. Pat insists that payment will be on the school.'

'Oh, thanks.'

'It's the least we can do. I told Pat about it. He was just amazed, said they'd have got away with it, too, if it hadn't been for you, the girl detective. Nothing's going to stop us now, is it?'

'No,' she smiled.

'Pat suggested that as you live opposite Neil, perhaps you could keep an eye on him for us?'

'Oh, right.' She hadn't expected this.

'Could you log down anything you see? Here, have a school exercise book.' He handed her a red exercise book and smiled winningly. 'Will you go on helping us?'

'Well, yes.' She was still a bit taken aback. 'It's just, I hardly know him, really.'

'Just make notes of anything you see at all,' said Josh.

'All right. So *I've* got my homework, then.'

'I'll check it every night,' said Josh.

The taxi arrived. Josh insisted on seeing her off.

He gave her a big two-armed wave. Happiness was just bursting out of him. And she had done that. He'd said he'd remember tonight for the rest of his life. She knew she would too.

Next morning at eight o'clock sharp, the stakeout began.

Mike Archer would, as usual, turn left out of his gate and walk past the bus shelter. Josh was sitting inside the shelter with two other Protectors, Alex and a new recruit, a fifth year called James. Josh would have liked to have had Andy in on this, but he lived too far away. He had let out a great whoop when Josh had rung to tell him the truth about Mike Archer's injury. He had nearly deafened Josh.

The bus shelter started to fill up with pupils from the two 'good schools' in the town. They waited in their uniforms, talking and laughing and directing glances at the three boys in black ties who sat hunched together. A few of the boys knew Josh and nodded to him. Then a pimply-faced boy asked what they were doing.

'Minding our own business,' growled Josh. If pupils obscured their view, Josh would mutter, 'Move it.'

More glances were directed at them, but Josh was always obeyed. There was something about these well-dressed, unsmiling boys that made everyone wary.

Josh had been afraid that Ally might turn up until he remembered that some days her mum gave her a lift to school. Two school buses wheezed up. There was the usual scrum to get on. More looks were directed at the Protectors and from the sanctuary of the bus, insults were called out.

Ten more minutes crawled by. Finally Mike Archer emerged from his house. Alex and James were on their feet. Josh cautioned them to wait. Mike's face looked normal. He must be going somewhere to 'make up'.

'I'd bet money he changes in that telephone box over there,' said Josh. He was right. Mike Archer got out a little pot of black dye and some bandages. Then he started putting the dye round his eye. He worked quickly, efficiently. It was like watching a professional. He was so intent on transforming himself that he didn't notice his audience at first. Then suddenly he looked up and almost fell over with shock. Alex and James started to laugh. All three swarmed into the telephone box. Mike attempted a smile, as if he was in on the joke too. 'Hello, lads,' he said.

'We've been waiting for you,' said Josh.

'Have you?' Mike tried to move further back. Instead he sent the black dye flying. It splattered down the window. 'Oops,' he said, attempting another smile. He took in the three grim faces. His smile vanished. 'Can't work out how you found out.' He was suddenly very polite.

'Did you really think you could fool us?' said Josh.

Mike began to gabble. He hadn't wanted to do this, but Neil had made him, he'd had no choice.

'This is so made up,' said Alex, aiming his fist at Mike. He would have hit him too if Josh hadn't stopped him.

Instead, Josh confiscated all Mike's bandages and make-up and said, 'You didn't need to do what Neil said. You could have come to us. The Protectors. You chose not to. Now you must take the consequences.'

Next day Mike arrived with a genuine black eye. At lunchtime he went to see Josh again, swearing he really had changed sides now and begging for protection.

Josh leaned right back in his leather chair. 'Normally we would give our help for nothing. But in your case you're going to have to prove to us you've changed sides. So we want you to carry on going round with Neil . . . but telling us everything you find out. I'm afraid you're going to have to continue as a double-agent for a bit longer.'

That afternoon, Ally arrived home to find a red rose waiting for her. There was a card too, it said:

Life without you is like a broken pencil. POINTLESS.

Love and stuff, J XX

A few days later, Ally returned from school to find a stranger sitting in her kitchen. Ally's mum was fussing about the woman. 'Now, are you sure you don't want another cup of tea?'

The woman had a thin, worn face and wispy, grey hair. She was wearing a large, white jumper and blue trousers. 'I couldn't drink another drop, thank you.' She looked frail but her voice was surprisingly deep.

Ally wondered if this was some aged relative of theirs she'd never met before. She looked at her again. The woman did seem vaguely familiar.

Then her mum said, 'Ally, you know Mrs Grey, Neil's mother, don't you?'

Now, of course, she recognised her. But before she'd never seemed quite real, glimpsed some way behind Neil in a hall which always reeked of polish. She was a shadowy, ghost-like figure, haunting rather than living in her house. Now she was smiling faintly at Ally and that was a relief as each night Ally had been spying on the house opposite, dutifully keeping a log of all Neil's movements. She'd feared Mrs Grey had spotted her and had come round to complain. Instead, Mrs Grey was saying, 'I never had the chance to thank you for all the shopping you got me. It was most kind.'

'Oh, any time,' said Ally. 'It's never a problem.' And she meant it. She felt protective towards this woman who had such a sad, faraway look in her eyes.

'I persuaded Mrs Grey to come round and have a cup of tea with me,' said her mum. Ally knew what an achievement that was. No one had seen Mrs Grey step out of her house for years.

'Are you sure you wouldn't like some more tea?' asked Ally.

'No, honestly. I really must go,' she replied.

'Oh, don't rush off,' began Ally's mum.

'Hardly that,' said Mrs Grey. 'I've been here since . . .' she peered at her watch. 'Goodness, I've been here for more than two hours. I've taken up far too much of your time.' She got to her feet. She was tiny, only coming up to Ally's shoulders. 'Goodbye, my dear,' she said. 'Lovely to have seen you.'

'Come back soon,' called Ally.

Ally heard her mum and Mrs Grey chatting in the hallway. If anyone could persuade Mrs Grey out into the world again it was her mum. She had a way with people. Perhaps because she never seemed critical of anyone. She just accepted them. Ally felt a glow of pride until she remembered something terrible. This woman, to whom she'd been so nice, was the mother of a terrible bully, who was also Josh's sworn enemy.

Ally's mother came back into the kitchen. 'That poor woman,' she said as she put the cups into the sink, 'I think she just wanted to talk, to unburden herself to someone. I couldn't believe some of the things she told me.'

'What kind of things?' asked Ally, her voice tight and controlled.

Ally's mum sighed, then switched the kettle on

again. It was nearly time for Dad's tea or 'wake-up call' as he dubbed it. 'Well, her husband used to beat poor Neil up regularly, you know. She told me that when Neil was no more than four, he was locked in a cupboard for hours. And then there were other things which she still can't bear to speak of. I feel so sorry for them both. 'Are you all right, love?'

Ally hesitated. Her mum was inviting her to feel sympathy for Neil. The whole idea seemed traitorous. 'Neil's not what you think, Mum.'

'What?'

'Well, we just see him doing his mum's shopping but he's also a first-class bully, you know.'

Ally's mum shook her head. 'That doesn't altogether surprise me. I've taught quite a few bullies over the years and I can tell you, they're all frightened little rabbits really, scared of the awful world around them and absolutely terrified of themselves and their vulnerability. That's got to be hidden at all costs. Most bullies are also victims, you know?'

'No, Mum, I'm sorry, but you can't just explain away all the damage Neil has done.'

'I'm not.'

'Yes you are, because Neil's had a few problems, that lets him off the hook. Neil's been bullying for years, you know. He's like some kind of bullying junkie. And he'll go on until someone stops him.'

'I'm not excusing Neil, I'm just saying that if we're judging him, he's starting from a different place to you and me. Inside his head he's probably going through hell.'

'So are his victims,' snapped Ally.

The phone rang. Ally's mum always rushed to the phone now as Sarah's baby was due any day. Ally hovered. It was Sarah but she had just rung up for a chat about her backache. Then the doorbell rang.

'Answer that, love,' Ally's mum mouthed. She was smiling. Ally still felt annoyed with her. Why did she keep trying to excuse Neil? He may have had some miserable times, but that didn't give him the right to inflict pain on other people, did it?

She opened the door. Neil was standing there. It was a tremendous shock. It was as if she'd been thinking about him so hard she'd conjured him up. Then she noticed he was carrying a large tin.

'Mum made you a cake, then forgot to bring it round. So here it is now.' In a kind of daze she took the tin from him and thanked him. She expected him to turn round and go, but he didn't. Close up, she noticed how pale his skin was. He looked as if he spent the whole of his life indoors. His eyes weren't so much cold as lifeless; he had very long eyelashes which gave his face an oddly feminine look. He was staring at Ally, as if expecting her to say something else.

'How's your Mum?' was the daft question she managed to ask at last.

He answered quite easily. 'Mum's having a rest. She gets tired very easily. It's all the medication she has to take, you see.'

Ally could only gape at him. This boy talking so anxiously about his mother didn't seem to have any connection with Josh's Neil.

'She finds lots of things very difficult, but she is getting better, slowly.'

'I'm glad,' said Ally. She thought of his mum caged up in that house and couldn't help feeling pity and sadness for her, for both of them.

'I'm trying to get her to go out more, but she gets very nervous.'

'Have you ever thought,' asked Ally, suddenly, 'of buying her one of those bleepers?'

'That's an idea,' said Neil.

'You can have them on a chain round your neck,

or anywhere, really. And if she ever needs help or feels worried, she can call someone right away.'

'I hadn't thought of that,' said Neil.

She and Neil were chatting like two friends. He was even trying to smile at her. But his smile never quite reached his eyes, which remained completely expressionless. Perhaps Neil didn't have any feelings? Or maybe he daren't ever show them after the horrors he had once seen? She suspected that those horrors would always be Neil's secret, shared only with his mum.

'I'll certainly tell Mum about the bleeper,' he said finally.

'Good, and thanks again for the cake.'

He walked four steps away then came back. 'Today meant such a lot to my mum. It was very nice of you.'

Maybe that was the biggest shock of all.

Nice wasn't a word she'd ever expected to hear Neil use.

Later that evening, Josh rang her. She told him all about talking to Neil and what her mum had said.

'All that concern for his mother. It's probably just an act.'

'Yes,' said Ally, but she was pretty certain it wasn't.

'Got your mum fooled, hasn't he?'

'My mum likes most people, especially those she thinks are underdogs.'

'Neil's not an underdog.'

'No, I know.'

'Neil might think he's a good guy because he does a bit of shopping for his mum. But then everyone thinks they're good guys really, I bet even Jack the Ripper did.'

Josh told her about Aaron, who had been summoned to a meeting with Neil. He didn't go and now his new bike was missing. Josh knew Neil had taken it: he operated from the bike racks, but they couldn't prove anything, of course. Aaron had also been warned to expect further 'hits'. The other boys, including Greg, had received warnings too. It was very tense at the moment. Josh went on and on.

Ally got the message. She felt ashamed of herself for softening towards Neil and for being disloyal to Josh. Afterwards she rushed upstairs and took up her observation post. She didn't see anything for ages. At last, the front door opened and there was Neil. He was carrying something. Ally strained forward. It was a clear evening so she should be able to make out what it was.

Suddenly Neil stopped and looked up at her house, her bedroom. She immediately sprang back, her heart hammering. Had Neil spotted her?

Ten

'We always take action against bullying,' spouted the headmaster. 'We think it's vital all our pupils feel valued.'

He beamed at the reporter.

'If he smiles much harder,' whispered Josh to Andy, 'he's going to burst right out of his suit.'

Wayne's mum had written to the local paper praising the wonderful scheme called the Protectors. 'Since the Protectors started, my son's whole attitude to school has changed.' It was the first good publicity the school had had in ages.

The paper was now running a feature on the Protectors, beginning with pictures and an interview with the headmaster in the school foyer. The

Protectors were hanging about there too. Not all of them. There were seventeen Protectors now. (Yesterday there'd been eighteen, but Josh had had to discharge one of them – a probationer – for starting a fight with one of Neil's gang.) Josh thought all of them together might look a bit intimidating, so there were just the six original Protectors, with him and Andy, of course.

The reporter, a youngish woman, friendly, but with eyes that didn't seem to miss much said, 'I suppose, Headmaster, the Protectors also highlight the bullying that exists here. You must be concerned about that?'

'Sneaky one,' murmured Andy.

But the headmaster didn't falter. 'Unfortunately, there is bullying in every school and many incidents go unreported. Here we're tackling the problem in a new and exciting way. That's why this venture has my full support and that of the school governors, who think the Protectors set such a good example by their concern for the school and their neat appearance.'

The reporter closed her book. 'Thank you very much. Now, if we could just take some more pictures and do our other interviews?'

'Of course,' said the headmaster. 'I'm sure you

will find everyone most co-operative. And please do not hesitate to call on me if you need any further information.'

Josh stepped forward. 'Excuse me, Sir, but it would be very useful if the Protectors had a bigger room of their own where they could meet and discuss their plans for the future.'

The headmaster was, for the first time, taken aback. 'Ah, yes, of course, we are rather tight for space, though.'

'But Mr O'Leary mentioned the old drama room which he says is never used these days.'

The reporter was looking interested now.

'Well, if Mr O'Leary has identified a room,' said the headmaster, 'I'm sure something can be arranged.'

'Thank you, Sir,' said Josh.

'Brilliant timing,' said Andy.

'It was Pat's idea.'

The photographer asked the boys to get into a line and smile. 'We don't do that sort of picture,' said Josh hastily. In the end Josh persuaded him to take pictures of the Protectors on patrol. Then Josh and Andy took the reporter to H.Q. and Josh saw the reporter noticing how pupils moved out of the way of the Protectors and rushed to hold doors open for them.

Outside H.Q. Greg was waiting to be interviewed. The headmaster had given strict instructions that Greg mustn't refer to anyone by name, nor must he say anything that could bring the school into disrepute. Despite this, Greg spoke simply and well.

After the reporter had left, Andy said, 'I thought she was going to burst out crying.'

'You had her in bits,' said Josh.

Greg smiled shyly. 'Well, it was all true. If it weren't for you two and the other Protectors, I'd be spending every day creeping round the school, just praying Neil and his gang wouldn't notice me.'

There was silence for a moment. 'You're worth more than that,' said Josh at last.

'I just can't believe how everything has changed,' went on Greg. 'I mean, last week I got one of Neil's notes and I did what you said, ignored it, and nothing happened. Nothing at all. I never ever see Neil now. It's all over, isn't it?'

Josh wasn't so sure about that. Neil was plotting something. But he didn't say this aloud.

Greg continued, 'And now I haven't got to worry about Neil, I feel so different: freer, as if I'm a new person.' He suddenly stopped, thinking he was saying too much and making a spectacle of himself. But Josh

162

knew exactly what Greg meant. In a way he felt new himself.

Greg stood up. 'How about if I get your lunch for you?'

'There's no need to do that,' began Andy.

But Josh interrupted. 'Are you sure?'

'Yes, of course. I can get someone to help me. Plenty of people in my form want to help the Protectors now.' He got his pad out, and like a proper waiter took down their order, waving away any talk of money. 'We'll settle-up later,' he said and rushed out.

'Would you believe it?' said Andy. 'That Greg would cut his arm off for you if you asked him. You've certainly made a difference to his life. Gives you a warm glow in here,' he tapped his chest, 'doesn't it?' He said this as a kind of joke. And Josh laughed. But he knew exactly what Andy meant.

There were two taps on the door. Then Lawrence walked in with a tallish, frightened-looking boy. 'I thought you ought to deal with this.'

The boy was wearing a tie. A thin, black tie.

'Thank you,' said Josh. 'We certainly will sort this out.'

Lawrence closed the door behind him. Josh glared at the boy. 'Why are you wearing a black tie?'

'I just felt like it.'

'Really,' said Josh. He leaned back in his leather chair, folding his arms. 'Are you aware that the black tie is the symbol of the Protectors?'

'Yes.'

'And did you know it's an offence to impersonate a Protector?'

'I wasn't exactly impersonating a Protector,' said the boy. 'I just think black ties look cool.'

'And one day I hope you'll be able to wear one legally, but not now. Is that clear?'

The boy nodded miserably. Josh looked at Andy.

'Take the tie off, please,' said Andy.

The boy obeyed at once.

'Now we *should* confiscate this tie,' said Andy. 'But do you promise never to wear it in the school grounds again?'

'Yes,' croaked the boy.

'Off you go then and don't let us ever catch you wearing that tie in future.'

The boy didn't go, though. He stood twisting the tie in his hands. 'Excuse me,' he murmured, 'what's the age when you can become a Protector?'

'Fourteen,' said Andy.

'But you never know, we might lower the age one

day, or maybe have a new special ranking, sub-Protectors or something,' said Josh. 'So watch out for more announcements.'

'I will. I like the idea of the Protectors.'

'So do we,' said Josh. 'Goodbye.'

The boy left.

'Did you know it's an offence to impersonate a Protector?' repeated Andy in Josh's grave tone. Then they both burst out laughing. They couldn't stop. They laughed until it hurt. They laughed the way they used to when they'd been messing about in a lesson and got away with it.

'This started out as just a skive,' said Andy. 'And now look at us, lording it about in here.'

'And today we've got a bigger room for the Protectors,' said Josh.

'We'll be running the school soon,' said Andy.

'We already are,' replied Josh, sinking back in his leather chair.

They laughed again.

It was the last lesson of the day.

'All right, fourth year, may I have your complete attention, please,' said Mr Denton. 'Everyone back to their seats and we'll hear your conclusions. Pass the stamps and pictures up to the front, please.' They had been discussing the different ways in which historical figures are portrayed.

All the pictures were handed to the front but no stamps. 'Stamps as well, please,' said Mr Denton. 'Come on, hurry up. All right, who's got my stamps?' His eyes panned the room but they settled on Neil.

'What are you looking at me for?' demanded Neil in his low, rusty voice.

'I'm not looking at anyone,' said Mr Denton. 'I just want those stamps back now. They're a vital part of my collection, been collecting since I was seven, you know. Come on, it's not even funny.'

Josh didn't like the way this was going. He shot an angry glance at Neil. What was he messing about with Denton's stamps for anyway? They would have absolutely no interest for Neil – unless he was planning to sell them.

'Look, come on.' Mr Denton's voice cracked with frustration. But no stamps appeared. 'All right,' Mr Denton slammed his folder of pictures down on the desk, 'if that's the way you want it. No one's leaving this room until I get those stamps back. Even if we have to stay here all night.'

'He's making things worse for himself,' hissed Andy.

Josh nodded grimly. You should never make wild threats you can't possibly keep. You undermine yourself right away.

'I'm waiting,' cried Mr Denton. Teachers shouldn't say that either, thought Josh. It makes them sound so feeble.

'All right, I left some of your exercise books behind in the staff room. I'm going to get them. I shall be away for just a minute. When I return, if those stamps are back on my desk, we'll say no more about it. You have my word on that. But if they're not, well . . .' Mr Denton was starting to splutter, 'Well, you'll all be very sorry. Is that clear?'

Relations had been rather strained between Josh and Mr Denton recently. Other teachers praised the Protectors and the way they were improving the image of the school, but Mr Denton still didn't really approve. When Josh had shown him the letter about the Protectors in the paper, he'd just said, 'I'm sorry, but I think there are very real dangers with this, too.' He had made Josh so angry. Even so, Josh took no pleasure from this scene. He shot to his feet, but he took care to speak easily, calmly. 'All the Protectors stand up, please.'

The other Protectors in the lesson – including Andy, Kane and Alex – looked puzzled, but each obeyed.

'Right, Neil, the Protectors are ordering you to hand the stamps over now.'

'Or what?' whispered Neil.

Josh kept his face impassive. Kane was already lumbering towards Neil. Alex followed him. They didn't say anything but they planted themselves either side of his table. Josh's face was as still as that of any poker player. So was Neil's. The rest of the class watched this duel fascinated. Then Neil turned very slowly towards Phil. He barely raised an eyebrow. A grin appeared on Phil's face as he dug into his jacket pocket and produced the stamps. He placed them on his desk without actually looking at them. He went on grinning without there being anything to grin about.

The stamps lay there until Kane picked them up and put them right in the middle of Mr Denton's desk. Without another word Josh sat down. The other Protectors followed. There were excited murmurs from the rest of the class.

Mr Denton returned. He saw at once that the stamps had been returned. He smiled with relief.

'The Protectors sorted that for you,' called out Josh. He didn't say that to show off – well not much – but just to demonstrate to Mr Denton the value of the Protectors: a proper, disciplined organisation, trying to right all the wrongs in the school. Instantly, the pleasure died out of Mr Denton's face. 'I see,' he said very quietly. Did being in the Protectors' debt make him feel less of a teacher? Josh could understand that. He wished he hadn't said anything now.

Afterwards, everyone was talking about how Josh had to sort out Mr Denton's class for him. 'It wasn't quite like that,' said Josh. But the rumour machine was in full swing.

Later, Josh sat in H.Q. 'I had to act when I did because Desert Head was just digging a bigger and bigger hole for himself. And he'd never have got those stamps back, would he?'

But Andy wasn't convinced. 'I don't think it was the Protectors' business. I mean, we weren't created to look after teachers. Also, you didn't consult anyone – like me – did you? You just went ahead.'

'There wasn't time. I had to move fast, otherwise there'd have been a major disaster.'

'Did you see the look Neil gave you?'

'Luckily I missed that.'

'Talk about death rays.'

'Seems like I'm crossed off his Christmas card list, then,' said Josh lightly.

Andy had to leave shortly after that to catch his bus. Josh stayed in H.Q. drinking a cup of coffee. He didn't want to go home yet. In fact, he didn't want to go home at all. Last night Lucy had had a big row with the alien. Of course Josh weighed in on her side but afterwards he told Lucy, 'Never let the alien see he's upset you. Don't give him the satisfaction. Always wear a mask when he's around.'

Josh's mum knew he was seeing Ally and kept on asking him to bring his 'girlfriend' round for a meal. 'Her family must be sick of the sight of you,' she said. She assumed he was round at his girlfriend's house every night. It was best she thought that. His mum wouldn't understand how much he liked H.Q. Just sitting in here seemed to clean his head out.

There was a knock on the door. Josh had been thinking so hard the noise made him jump. 'Come in.' He wondered if it was Mr Denton. It was Mike.

'Can I speak to you, please?' he asked very respectfully.

'Of course,' said Josh. But he didn't ask Mike to

sit down. He stared rather coldly at him. He still didn't trust him.

'Everyone's talking about what you did in Desert Head's class.'

Josh nodded impatiently.

'You know you said to contact you when I had some news?'

'Yes.'

'Well, I've just overheard Neil plotting something. He was with a whole group of them.'

'Go on.'

'I couldn't make out very much, they were whispering – I think they're becoming suspicious of me.'

'Everyone's suspicious of you,' said Josh dryly. 'What have you to tell me?'

'Well, they're going to strike soon.'

'Are they?'

'They want you to think they're going after Greg or one of the people you're protecting. But really . . . You're the target.'

Josh kept his face calm. 'Tell me more.'

'It's either you, or someone very close to you.'

Josh immediately thought of Ally. He was nervous about her living so close to Neil. Especially after Ally thought he might have spotted her spying on him. She would make the ideal victim for Neil. He sat up. 'Okay, now I want details.'

'I don't know any. That's all I heard.'

'So you've only got half the tale? Useless.' Josh wouldn't normally have been so abrupt, but he didn't like Mike and he was feeling suddenly very tired and weary.

'I just wanted to warn you,' said Mike.

'You've done it. Goodnight.'

Eleven

Ally stepped into the taxi. The driver recognised her. 'Home?' he said.

'Home,' she repeated with a smile. Once she'd have thought it so strange never going round to a boyfriend's house, never seeing his family. Yet, in such a short time, she'd become used to meeting Josh at H.Q. And in a way, Pat, the caretaker, and his wife, Marie, were like Josh's other family: fussing over him and last night inviting him and Ally round for a meal at their house just inside the school grounds.

Marie had taken out the family albums, despite her husband's cry of, 'They won't be interested in those.'

Josh and Ally poured over every snap.

Tonight, though, it had just been her and Josh in H.Q. Josh had been very grave at first, warning her to be on her guard against Neil. But Ally didn't think she had anything to fear from him. Although she and Neil hadn't chatted since their conversation on the doorstep, he'd always waved in a very friendly way.

'Why don't we have a break from all this?' she said. So he tested her on her part in *A Taste of Honey*. He played all the other roles and was remarkably good.

'You should act, too,' said Ally.

'I spend my whole life acting,' replied Josh. 'Still, Andy says he can tell when I'm play acting.'

'How?'

Josh grinned. 'He says I look all constipated.'

'But don't you always?' she teased.

'You will pay for that,' said Josh. Then he started waving a ticket in the air. It was a ticket for *A Taste of Honey* next week. He'd got a front row seat. 'I'm going to cheer every time you come on,' he said.

'You'd better not put me off.'

Josh only laughed.

It had been a lovely evening and a perfect antidote to the day's highly dramatic start: the phone ringing at half-past six in the morning. Ally's sister had just been rushed to hospital, the baby was due any time. Much frantic activity. Mum dashed away. Dad wasn't home yet, of course. Later Mum rang her at school. 'You're an auntie,' she said, 'a little girl. Mother and baby doing wonderfully well.' Mum was staying over for a couple of days and Dad was going to try to get some time off work. But in the end he couldn't.

'I'll be fine in the house on my own,' said Ally. But Dad had to go and see one of their neighbours, Mrs Jones, to ask her to keep an eye on Ally.

When she arrived home, to her great irritation she discovered Mrs Jones standing outside her house. As she got closer to Mrs Jones she wasn't irritated any more, she was scared.

'Is it my sister? Is she all right?'

'Oh yes, my dear.'

'And the baby?'

'They're both fine. Your mother's left you a message, I think.' Then Mrs Jones became embarrassed, uneasy. 'I'd just popped round to see if you were all right, when I saw this.' Perhaps because it was dark, Ally didn't take in anything strange at first. Then the words jumped out at her. They were written in red capital letters across the front door:

She flinched as if she'd been struck. Tears of rage filled her eyes.

'It can't have been up long, only a couple of hours,' said Mrs Jones. 'It's not chalk, otherwise I'd have rubbed it off right away. It's been done with one of those felt pens which won't come off.'

Suddenly Ally remembered that Neil had used one of those felt pens when he'd trashed H.Q.

'It's disgusting, it should be reported,' said Mrs Jones.

'It will be,' replied Ally. She fumbled for her key. She charged into the house and immediately dialled the number of Josh's school. She knew it by heart now.

Pat answered. Yes, Josh was still there.

'What's up?' She told him the words which were on her front door. 'It must be Neil. I'll be right over.'

'There's no need,' she began, but he'd already rung off. And actually, she wanted him there so badly.

Mrs Jones hovered. 'Who did you ring, dear?'

'Someone who'll sort this out.'

'Do you know who did this?'

'Oh, yes.'

'I think you've got a message,' said Mrs Jones. The red light on the answer phone was winking away. Would that be Neil boasting about what he'd done? She felt sick.

It was her mum, bright and cheerful. 'Just to tell you the baby is absolutely lovely and all is well.'

She pictured her mum returning to see that vile message all over the front door, scrawled by the boy she'd tried to defend. Now her mum would discover what he was really like. She'd realise there wasn't good in everyone. As for her dad, she imagined him coming home from work at eight o'clock tomorrow morning. Her dad had lived here for thirty years. Why did Neil have to write such evil things? Her anger was like a pain deep inside her stomach. She had to sit down.

'Tomorrow we'll paint over that . . .' Mrs Jones said.

'I've got to paint over it tonight,' said Ally. 'My parents mustn't see it.'

'No, they shouldn't,' replied Mrs Jones. 'Especially on such a happy day as this.'

A car pulled up noisily.

Ally ran to the front door. Josh and Marie were

already out of the car and staring at the message on her door. Marie came into the house, loudly declaring her sympathy and anger. Josh gave Ally's hand a squeeze. They all walked into the kitchen. Mrs Jones was introduced to everyone, then seemed to melt into the background, intimidated by the two strong new personalities in the house.

'So, you know who did this?' said Marie.

'Neil.' Josh didn't need to add a surname. 'He lives opposite Ally. This is his idea of revenge against the Protectors.'

'It's boys like him,' said Marie, 'who pull our school down to the bottom of the league table. That Neil's had so many warnings too, but I think he's a lettuce short of a salad.'

Josh smiled grimly.

'The headmaster said one more bad thing and out Neil goes,' went on Marie.

'Well, here is the bad thing,' said Josh. 'But it would be very difficult to prove. Neil always covers his tracks.'

'He might even have got someone else to do this for him,' said Marie. 'Anyway, Josh said you'd need green paint and that's what I've brought. Do you want us to start now?'

'Yes please.'

So, at ten o'clock that night, Josh and Marie set about painting the door. Other neighbours came out to watch, tut-tutting over what had been written. Lights appeared in all of the houses – except one.

'He doesn't need to see what he's done,' said Ally. 'I'd like to march into that house now . . .'

'No, don't do anything yet,' said Josh. 'He's used you to get at me. I'll settle it.' There was a tightness in Josh's voice, as if he could barely hold in his anger. 'Tomorrow I'm holding a meeting: a Council of War. Everyone wants Neil out of the school – well, the Protectors are the ones to do just that. Neil is going to regret bitterly what he's done tonight.'

Greg felt honoured that he was allowed to attend the Council of War. It was because he'd helped set up the old drama studio, which was now the Protectors' common room. This was the first time they'd used it. Josh and Andy sat right in the centre of the semi-circle. Behind them was a big blow-up of the newspaper article about the Protectors, entitled, 'The Pupils Who Help Each Other.' Josh had crossed out the inaccuracies such as 'The Protectors are voluntary prefects'. But the photos of them in action were excellent. Josh had ordered a full set to be displayed all over the room.

'Surprised you didn't bring your leather chair with you,' called out Kane.

'Now there's an idea,' grinned Josh. But the rest of the meeting was deadly serious.

'Neil knows how to take you by surprise,' said Josh, 'I'll give him that, but I will not rest while he is walking round this school.'

At first all the talk was of fighting Neil, of 'giving him a good kicking'. But Josh said that was only a last resort. 'The Protectors don't go round kicking people, they've too much class for that. There must be a better way of destroying him.'

Most of the Protectors longed for combat, but Josh had appeased them for the moment. He called for suggestions. 'Everyone's got to turn away from him,' said a new Protector, 'act as if he doesn't exist, as if he's invisible. We've got to get the whole school to do it.'

Josh thought that was a good idea, but added gloomily, 'The trouble is, no one talks to him much now.'

Someone else suggested putting Neil's name down for litter duty, dinner duty, making an appointment for him to see the school nurse . . . 'make sure every spare moment he has is occupied with things he doesn't want to do.' This idea was widely liked and was undoubtedly the best suggestion.

'I still don't see how this is going to make him leave,' said Alex. 'In the end we're going to have one massive fight with him and his gang.'

'No,' cried Josh. 'Look, when I leave this school I want to pass the Protectors on, so I don't want any loose cannons messing things up'. He stared at Alex. 'Believe me, I want Neil out of this school more than anyone else here. But there's got to be a better way than just getting into a massive scrum.'

'The fight could be out of school,' said Alex, as an afterthought. There were ripples of agreement. But Josh only frowned. He brought the evening to an end. But no one was satisfied.

Greg walked along the corridor thinking about the meeting. He'd really thought Neil had been defeated. Instead, he'd just been biding his time and had come back more vindictively than ever. Inside his head, Greg let out a great roar of anger and frustration. He felt as shaky as the day he'd stood outside Smedleys.

He leaned against the wall and saw some people

leave Mr Denton's stamp club meeting. If it hadn't been for the meeting with the Protectors, Greg would have been at that. He was about to tell Mr Denton that he'd attend the next meeting when the teacher shot past him.

Greg peered round the empty classroom. Mr Denton's stamps were laid out on the desk. It was then that Greg had an idea. A cold shiver ran through him. He could never do it. Yet, it would be in a brilliant cause, and no harm would come to the stamps. He stood there, stunned by his plan. But he mustn't hesitate. He reached forward, swept the stamps into his case, then ran out of the classroom.

'It's a great idea and it might just work,' said Josh.

Greg beamed.

Josh looked round at the three other Protectors in H.Q. Andy, Kane and Alex. Alex was a last minute addition at Kane's suggestion. He said Alex could break into any locker in less than ten seconds.

Kane and Alex nodded in agreement. 'Sorry, but I'm not too keen on the plan,' said Andy. He spoke in a low voice and was staring at Josh.

'Why not?' asked Josh.

'It's a bit snidey.'

'Snidey.' Alex pounced on the word.

Andy went on talking to Josh. 'At our meeting we said we didn't want to get into fighting. We'd only devalue the Protectors. Well this plan devalues the Protectors too. Really, we're just fitting-up people.'

'Neil isn't a person,' said Alex. 'I bet he hasn't even got a pulse.'

Kane laughed loudly.

'Now, this is strictly a one-off,' said Josh.

'People always say that,' said Andy.

'If I say it's a one-off, that's what it will be.' Then, in a more placatory tone, 'All we're doing is turning Neil's reputation against him: stealing Denton's stamps is exactly the kind of thing Neil would do. We're just anticipating him and giving the school a perfect excuse to expel him. Then mission accomplished, and everyone's happy.'

'Except Denton, when he discovers his stamps are missing,' said Andy.

'Yeah, but he'll get his stamps back,' said Josh. 'He'll have a few minutes' trauma but then he'll be okay and he'll never have to put up with Neil in his class again. We're saving him hours of misery.'

'I say we just get on with it,' said Alex. 'We haven't got much time left.'

'I agree,' said Kane.

Josh turned to Andy. 'What about you?'

'I am your bondsman and must obey.' Andy spoke as if he were making a joke, only Josh knew how devastating Andy's comment was: Andy was acting as if he was just another Protector. But he'd never been that: he was the co-founder, Josh's partner, a partner who sat on a school chair rather than a leather one, but a partner none the less.

'I am your bondsman and must obey.' That was a pathetic thing to say. Very snidey, too. And so heavy-handed. Josh turned to Andy, expecting him to say something else. He almost wanted him to. But he didn't say another word, just sat there grinding his teeth. Andy couldn't stand being wrong. That's why he was acting like this. He was the one playing games, not Josh.

'We've got about four minutes left before school starts again,' said Alex. 'Are we doing anything or just talking about it?'

'The Protectors are men of thought as well as men of action,' said Josh. 'But yes, we are doing something. Greg, will you give Alex the stamps?' Alex reached out and snatched them.

Josh continued, 'Alex, you will break into Neil's

locker, place the stamps inside, then lock it again. There shouldn't be anyone about until the bell goes. If there is, can you distract them, Kane?'

'No problem.'

'Andy and I will be outside.' He looked at Andy who just went on grinding his teeth. 'We'll make sure no one else comes in and disturbs you. Greg, will you go to Mr Denton's classroom? He'll probably be going ape now wondering where his stamps are. I want you to slip into the conversation that you saw Neil hanging about. Don't tell Denton at first, and tell him reluctantly. Let him think he's forced this information out of you.'

Kane and Alex were already on their feet.

'We mustn't tell anyone else what we're doing,' said Josh. 'Not even any of the other Protectors. Any questions?'

'No time,' said Alex.

'Okay,' said Josh. 'If this works we'll have rid the school of Neil forever and done everyone here a massive favour. One day they'll probably erect statues to us.'

Everyone grinned, except Andy.

'Good luck,' said Josh. 'Let's go to war.'

*

Greg spotted Mr Denton walking down the corridor, he rushed after him and followed him into the classroom.

'Hello, Greg,' said Mr Denton cheerily. 'You waiting to see me?'

'Yes, Sir.'

'I've just had my bank manager apologise to me and it was marvellous. I've been chasing my bank for weeks. Now, finally, they've admitted they've been wrong . . . wonderful.' He looked as if he was about to burst into song. 'Anyway, what can I do for you?'

'I just wanted to say sorry I missed the stamp club today and can I still join?' asked Greg.

'Of course you can,' began Mr Denton. For the first time he looked down at his desk. 'My stamps. I left them here. I should have locked the door, but I was only gone . . .' He peered at Greg, his face a picture of distress.

'Is anything wrong, Sir?' asked Greg.

'Yes, Greg, something is very wrong: all the stamps I brought in for the stamp club have gone, vanished,' his voice fell, 'been stolen, I suppose.'

Greg found it hard to look at Mr Denton. He reminded himself of what Josh had said, he'll have a few minutes' trauma then he'll never have to put up with Neil in his class again. Mr Denton kept staring at the desk as if he were expecting the stamps to materialise. 'I know I left them here. So someone's come in . . . Greg, you didn't spot anyone in here, did you?'

Greg hesitated just as he'd been told. 'Er . . .'

'I'm not asking you to tell tales, Greg, but this stamp collection is quite valuable and it means a lot to me. If someone has stolen it I've still got a chance of catching him, if you'll help me.'

Slowly, as if the information was being dragged out of him, Greg began, 'Well, yes, I did see someone come out of the classroom.'

'Who was it, Greg?'

'It wasn't anyone from my year, he was older.'

'And was he carrying anything?'

'I don't think so . . . I'm really not sure.'

'All right. Do you know his name?'

'Yes I do, he's called Neil.'

'Neil.' Mr Denton spat the word out. Then he thumped the table. Greg jumped back in alarm. Mr Denton quickly recovered himself. 'It's all right, I'll take over now and I will keep your name out of this. Don't worry.'

The bell rang. Greg walked to the door.

'Greg.'

He stopped.

'I know what you've just done wasn't easy, but you have done the right thing. Thank you.'

Greg nodded solemnly.

Outside in the corridor someone hissed his name. It was Alex. Greg looked up at him. 'Everything go all right in there?'

'Fine, I . . .'

'It's all right, I know what you did. Well, the stuff is where it should be, looks like your plan might just work.' Alex stomped away.

Greg stood thinking. If his plan worked then he, Greg, would be the one who'd got rid of Neil. A delicious chill ran through him. He'd never felt so alive.

It was registration, but today the register lay unmarked on the desk. Mr Denton was walking round his classroom. He told them about the missing stamps. He told them that someone from his form had been seen leaving the room just when the stamps disappeared.

'If I get the stamps back now, I shall assume someone here got a bit over-enthusiastic and borrowed them without telling me. That will be the end of the matter. I promise.' He stared round hopefully. 'Has anyone borrowed my stamps by accident?'

Complete silence. A large smirk crossed Alex's face. Josh frowned at him. They mustn't do anything to draw attention to themselves. Mr Denton finally picked up the register. He rushed through the names, his mind clearly elsewhere. Then people started to get up.

'Sit down, everyone,' said Mr Denton. 'No one is to leave until I say so. Now, I shall take the register to the staffroom while you all wait here.'

'Leaving it to the Protectors again, are you?' sneered Neil.

Mr Denton shot him a look of undiluted hatred. 'No I am not. I am giving the person who took the stamps one last chance to return them. If the stamps are back on my desk when I come back, then I shall say no more about it. If they are not, then I shall take further action.'

There were cries of, 'Oooh, I'm so scared,' from Neil's cronies.

Mr Denton left.

Heads swivelled round. Any break in the school routine was welcome but no one quite knew what to make of this. People stared questioningly at each other. 'Looks like a job for the Protectors,' called a voice from the back.

Suddenly everyone was staring at Josh. 'Denton said he wants to deal with this one,' said Josh. 'So I'm going to let him . . . but I do think it's a bit pathetic stealing the guy's stamps.'

'Yeah, go on, give them back to Desert Head,' called someone, 'before he bursts into tears.' There were sniggers, but murmurs of agreement too.

Now everyone was eyeballing Neil. He didn't say a word.

'He looks guilty as hell,' whispered Josh to Andy.

Andy didn't reply, just breathed heavily through his mouth. He still had a face on him. Josh hated it when Andy sulked. It was so boring.

Mr Denton returned. He immediately took in the empty desk. He squared his shoulders, then planted himself in the middle of the classroom. At last he was acting like a proper teacher, thought Josh.

'Now I will search all your bags. Please have them ready.' He walked round the room, polite but very serious. The whole class waited for him to reach Neil. He didn't have a proper bag, just a carrier bag. It took Mr Denton about four seconds to rifle through its contents. He walked slowly back to his desk. Josh's heart beat faster. Mr Denton must have a locker search now.

The teacher faced the class. If only Josh could prompt him, but he didn't dare. Mr Denton's face was burning. 'Has anyone any objections if I check their lockers?'

Josh could have laughed with relief. Neil gave one of his short laughs, he obviously found this whole charade highly amusing. He won't be laughing soon, thought Josh.

The class filed down the corridor to the lockers. 'I'll explain to your teachers why you're late,' said Mr Denton. 'I'm sure they'll understand.' Mr Denton couldn't be seen to pick on Neil, so they all stood in front of their lockers which were in alphabetical order. Neil's was the eighth on the list. Kane, Josh and Alex were all standing together. Andy was a little way from them. It seemed to take each boy ages to open his locker, digging into his pockets for keys, then bringing out the wrong one.

Then came Neil's turn. He ambled towards his. He had his key in his hand. Slowly, lazily, he opened it.

Mr Denton reached inside. His hand stopped. Then

he pulled out what looked like a tiny scrap of paper, then another and another. They looked like pieces of a jigsaw. His four pages of stamps had been ripped to pieces. The whole class was deathly silent. Josh turned furiously to Alex. 'Had to be done,' mouthed Alex. 'Explain later.'

Mr Denton turned to Neil. 'Did you do this?'

'No.'

'How did they get into your locker, then?'

Neil shrugged. If he was shocked by the stamps turning up in his locker, he didn't show it.

'You were seen leaving my room when I was away. What have you to say to that?'

Neil shrugged again. He could reply, 'I'm innocent', but Josh knew Neil wouldn't lower himself. Nothing, not even wrongful arrest, would be allowed to crack Neil's shell.

'Don't just stand there shrugging your shoulders at me.' Mr Denton's voice suddenly broke. 'Those stamps were precious – yet you had to destroy them. Why? What good does it serve anyone ripping them to bits? Answer me . . .'

Neil didn't reply, he just smiled. That smile was like a big guilty sign round his neck. It sent Mr Denton over the top. 'All right, go and stand outside the headmaster's office now. Go on, get out of my sight.'

Neil slouched his way past everyone. Mr Denton started picking up the bits of stamps. Some dropped on to the floor. Josh bent down and helped him.

'All right, everyone, off to your classrooms,' said Mr Denton.

The class left slowly. For once, practically everyone was on the teacher's side. All the comments were about Neil and what a sicko he was.

Josh said quietly, 'Are you all right, Mr Denton?'

'Yes, I'm all right,' replied the teacher equally quietly. He smiled. 'Josh, will you do me a favour? There'll be a class waiting in my room, will you ask Mrs Scott – she'll be next door – to keep an eye on them, and tell the class to check over their essays? I shouldn't be long.'

'Of course, Sir,' said Josh.

Mr Denton patted Josh on the shoulder and walked quickly away.

Alex and Kane were waiting for him. Andy was hovering too. 'What do you think you're playing at?' demanded Josh. 'We never said anything about tearing the stamps up.'

Alex looked nervous but defiant. 'We had to push

Denton right to the edge. We don't want any more last chances for Neil, do we?'

'But those stamps were worth a lot of money,' said Josh.

'Then we'll have a collection for him,' replied Alex flippantly. 'Besides, tearing those stamps up is exactly what Neil would have done.'

'You acted right outside your jurisdiction,' snapped Josh. He pressed his face close to Alex's. He could hardly contain his fury. 'You can't make a decision like that on your own.'

'I had no choice,' said Alex, glaring furiously back at Josh. They were on the brink of a fight.

'I think what Alex did was very necessary,' said Kane suddenly and there was just a hint of menace in his voice.

Almost instinctively, Josh looked round for Andy. He'd gone. He stared again at Kane and Alex. They couldn't have stood much closer together. Josh knew he couldn't push this confrontation any further, not here, anyhow. He had to rein in his anger. He took a deep breath, 'We'll discuss this later.'

Neil didn't appear for the rest of the afternoon. Mr Denton seemed to have vanished too.

'I'll see if I can find out anything,' Josh said to Kane. He was still smarting about the way Alex had torn up the stamps without consulting him. He felt Alex was trying to hijack the Protectors. It was time for Josh to reassert his authority.

However, just before lessons finished, Josh was summoned to the secretary's office. There was an urgent phone call for him. Without quite knowing why, Josh felt scared.

He walked into the secretary's office which was next door to the headmaster's, only her door was made of glass. She smiled at Josh. Was that a bad sign?

He picked up the phone. 'Hello?'

'Josh, it's me.'

It was Ally.

'What's happened?' He was panicking. Had she been attacked?

'Nothing, except Mrs Jones has just come up to the school to tell me they've found the boys who wrote on my door and they aren't anything to do with Neil.'

'How do you know?'

'Because they'd gone round writing racist rubbish on other people's doors too, but the police caught them this lunchtime. Mrs Jones says they've admitted it.'

There was a slight pause. 'Interesting,' said Josh at last.

'But look, this changes things, doesn't it? There's no need to carry on with your plan to get Neil out of your school.'

Josh said nothing.

'I'd feel dreadful if you did. Please, Josh, leave things for now.'

'Look, I'm afraid I've got to go,' said Josh. 'I'll come round tonight.'

'Yes, all right.'

'Thanks for calling. Bye.'

His throat felt very tight. So Neil was innocent. Today he'd been punished for a crime he didn't commit. It didn't make any sense. Josh frowned with annoyance. How could Neil not have written that message? He had to be involved somehow. He was certainly guilty of other crimes against innocent people. Stacks of them. Anyway, it was too late now. The wheels of justice were already in motion.

Outside the secretary's office, Pat was waiting for him. He signalled to Josh to come over. 'This is all unofficial, mind, but I think our friend Neil's about to get his comeuppance at last ... stole a teacher's stamp collection and then destroyed it.'

'I know,' began Josh.

'Well, he'll be suspended and I think it's very likely he'll be out this time. They always get too confident, don't they? Always get caught in the end.' He gave Josh the thumbs up and disappeared.

So this was it: victory. It looked like he'd really got rid of Neil. Josh should be celebrating. Well, of course he was pleased. After all, he'd got the result he wanted, but not the way he wanted. Andy was right: they had just fitted-up Neil today. And that went against the whole spirit of the Protectors.

The headmaster's door opened.

Josh saw Mr Denton leave. He went up to him, giving him a friendly smile. 'Hello, Sir, we wondered ...'

'Neil's been suspended,' said Mr Denton slowly. 'Any further action is up to the governors.'

'That's good,' said Josh.

Mr Denton didn't reply for a moment, then suddenly, confidingly, 'This is just between ourselves for now, but I've also handed in my notice.'

Josh stared at him incredulously. 'Why?'

Mr Denton laughed. 'I should think that's obvious.

What happened today was partly my fault.'

'But that's rubbish, Sir,' exclaimed Josh. 'Some-one steals your property, that's not your fault.'

'Yes it is. I didn't lock my door, I put temptation in someone's way. I didn't think like a teacher. Actually, I've been thinking about moving for a while. Today just gave me the jolt I needed.'

'But you can't go. You're a good teacher.'

'Thank you, Josh. You saying that means a lot to me. But it's not enough, is it? You've got to be a good policeman as well – but you knew that all along, didn't you? Anyway . . . I've enjoyed teaching you, Josh.' He gave a strange kind of smile, then he turned away. 'Got to go now. See you tomorrow.' He rushed away before Josh could say anything else.

Josh walked quickly towards H.Q. He felt sick inside. He hadn't meant this to happen at all. Mr Denton couldn't leave. Josh had to talk him out of it. If only he'd kept a tighter grip on things, on Alex.

He passed Andy. 'Kane and Alex are waiting for you at H.Q.,' said Andy in a low monotone.

'Neil's been suspended; they think he'll probably be expelled,' replied Josh as triumphantly as he could.

'Congratulations,' said Andy. There wasn't a note of congratulation in his voice.

'Not really,' said Josh.

Andy looked at him.

'Denton's just told me he's resigned. He said today was the last straw.'

'We'll talk him round.'

Suddenly he sounded like the old Andy again.

'You were right,' said Josh quietly. 'Today was too underhanded for a Protector's operation.'

Andy looked surprised at this admission, but pleased. 'We've got rid of Neil, anyhow,' he said.

Josh nodded.

'That's something . . . a lot.'

'Yeah, sure.'

'And if Alex hadn't been so keen on the plan I might have liked it a bit more.'

Josh frowned. 'We're going to have to watch Alex . . . He could be trouble.'

'He is trouble,' said Andy.

'He should have obeyed my instructions today, not gone off and . . . he's to blame for Mr Denton leaving.'

Andy murmured in agreement.

'Are you coming back to H.Q.?' asked Josh.

'I would, but if I don't catch this bus . . .'

'There's not another one for two weeks. I know.'

'I'll give you a bell tonight.'

'You'd better,' said Josh.

Andy suddenly held out his hand as if he'd just met Josh for the first time.

Josh took it and didn't let go of it for ages.

Josh was telling Ally about today. About Neil. And she wasn't saying a word. She was just sitting there. They were in her house, sitting at the table. They had the house to themselves as her dad was at work and her mum was still with Sarah.

She'd made lots of sandwiches and there was a plateful of chocolate biscuits; she knew how fond Josh was of chocolate. But Josh was too busy talking to eat. He wanted to get this bit over with. Ally wasn't eating either. She was just staring at him. She looked funny.

He stopped. Something was wrong. 'Well, go on, say something.' He laughed uneasily.

'I don't believe you.'

'It's all true.'

'I don't believe you did that.' She was glaring at him now. 'You'd no right to plant things on Neil. Just who do you think you are?'

'Me? I'm just a very exceptional person.' But this

time she had a face of stone. He turned away from her. He stared out of the window at Neil's house. Although his curtains were drawn, Neil could take a peek at this unhappy scene any time he wanted. Josh got up. 'All right if I pull the curtains?'

'Guilty conscience?'

'I just want a little privacy.' He fumbled about trying to find the string. He pulled the curtains together. They were practically in darkness now, there was just one lamp on. He sat down again. His head was throbbing.

This should have been one of his greatest moments. He'd defeated Neil. Alex and Kane were certainly happy about it. Earlier he'd had a celebration with them in H.Q. Kane had kept on about the 'master stroke' of tearing up the stamps, while Alex had looked so smug and cocky that Josh had realised he didn't like either of them very much.

Josh reached out and took a chocolate biscuit. He laughed. 'Ally, will you stop looking like I've just murdered your budgie.'

'Sorry, I'm just stunned by what you've told me.'

'Oh, come on. I think you're being a bit silly about this. You've got to remember, Neil was on his last warning. He'd have been chucked out of school sooner or later. We just made sure it's sooner: and stopped any more bullying or writing on doors.'

'Just to remind you, Neil didn't write on my door.'

'We don't know that for certain.'

'Someone else has already admitted it.'

'He could still be behind it.'

She let out a cry of exasperation. 'He's innocent!'

Josh was getting angry now. He slammed the biscuit down on his plate. 'Let me just remind you about Neil: his main hobby is seeking out people to hurt. These people have done nothing to him but he plots to humiliate and finally destroy them. I can't tell you how many lives he's ruined and now you're asking me to feel sorry that he got a dose of his own medicine today?' He paused, his head was killing him. 'Anyway, if it hadn't been for you, today would never have happened.'

That made her stop in her tracks. Josh watched her with a kind of grim satisfaction. 'Last night you rang me wanting help. I rushed round with Marie. And when I saw what he'd done to you I was so angry, I had to take revenge right away. I did it for you, Ally, and that's the truth.'

'So it's all my fault?' There was a strangeness to her voice he didn't like.

'No, no, what I'm saying is, you inspired me today.'

She got to her feet slowly and in the same, strange voice said, 'So, if I'm responsible I'd better go round to Neil's house and apologise to him . . . now.'

Josh staggered to his feet. He felt sick and scared. 'On no account are you to go to his house and apologise to someone so completely evil . . .'

'You can't stop me. I'm not one of your Protectors.'

His heart was hammering. He started shouting as if to drown out the sound. 'If you go round to his house now, we're finished. Do you hear me?' Something inside him told him to stop shouting, not to make these wild threats. He was doing it all wrong. But the words continued to tear out of him. 'I came round here expecting, well at least a bit of gratitude, a bit of loyalty. Instead, I get . . . Do what you like, I'm out of here.' He hesitated, waiting for her to say something, to stop him. But she wasn't even looking at him.

He stormed past her. The cold air hit him. He stumbled along, hardly seeing where he was going. He was upset and angry. He couldn't believe Ally's behaviour tonight. The way she'd sat there, looking at him as if he were her worst enemy. The way she'd kept defending Neil. The way she'd let him go. Then he thought about himself: last night he'd only wanted to protect her. Now he just wanted to make her feel bad. It was unravelling. This whole relationship. And all the time he was away from her it would go on unravelling. He had to go back to her now. He'd admit things had gone too far today: something about the plan hadn't felt right. He'd admitted that much to Andy. Then, maybe, he'd start to get her back.

He began to run towards her house again. He was nearly crying. He reached the top of her road. Then he stopped. In a night full of nasty shocks, this was the nastiest of all. He turned back, still not able to take in what he'd seen: Ally, standing outside Neil's house. It hadn't been an idle threat. She really was grovelling to Neil. Well, that was it, she was a traitor and she'd never see him again. Not that she would care. He squinted at his watch. It wasn't too late to go to H.Q.

He ran harder and harder. But he still couldn't stop crying.

Josh would never have to see Neil at school again. All day he had to keep telling himself this. He had to keep cheering himself up. It was stupid, hadn't he won?

Lunchtime was mad. There was a line of people outside his door, all wanting to join the Protectors – or help the Protectors.

'We'll be signing up half the school at this rate,' said Andy.

'We're going to have to be more selective,' said Josh. 'Get better people this time.'

'We recruited a bit too quickly before.'

'We had no choice. We had this massive problem dropped into our laps, called Neil. Now we can take our time, screen everyone and phase a few of the Alex's out too.'

'We'll never get rid of Alex now,' said Andy.

'If we have to we will,' replied Josh. But he was feeling distinctly edgy. He had a horrible feeling events were slipping away from him.

Greg brought their lunches in. He did this every day now, always acted like it was a great honour to be allowed to do it. Just when they had started to eat, in marched Alex and Kane. Fake smiles all round.

Alex had seen all the potential new recruits and he figured that soon the Protectors would need 'a new chain of command'. He licked his lips every time he said the phrase. He clearly saw himself as part of it, so did Kane.

Andy was bristling, getting angry but Josh quickly cut in. 'That's a really interesting idea. We'll get back to you soon. Thanks for bringing it to our attention.'

Afterwards he explained to Andy, 'We mustn't say anything. Don't let them know what we're thinking. Keep them guessing.' But Josh was worried. He was going to have to get some more allies, start plotting.

After school, Josh sat in H.Q. having a cup of coffee. This was one of his favourite times of the day. Sometimes Pat popped in. Today it was Alex. He didn't want to rush Josh, but had he thought any more about his idea? Josh played for time, promising a meeting soon. He didn't want to go home but he did want to get rid of Alex.

He locked up H.Q. and he and Alex walked into the reception. All the Protectors used this entrance now. Pat rushed over to them gasping for breath. Josh looked at him in alarm. 'What's wrong, Pat?'

'That boy's back here. I was just outside when that Neil came up out of nowhere on a moped. He started tearing about the place like a bat out of hell. I told him to stop but he just laughed. Then he came charging towards me. I had to jump into a bush.'

Josh smothered a grin. The idea of Pat leaping

into a bush was funny or it would have been if Neil hadn't been involved. Pat seemed to recover himself. 'There are no senior staff on the premises so it's up to me to take action. I'm going to call the police. You both stay here. That boy belongs in a straitjacket.'

Josh said to Alex, 'We're not hiding away in here from Neil, are we?' Actually, Josh could have waited in there very easily. But it was a point of honour. If they sheltered inside, Neil had won after all.

They stepped outside. It had been raining all day and now it was grey and drizzly and already quite dark. The posse of boys who usually hung round the school entrance loomed ahead of them, completely blocking the path leading out of the school. They saw Josh and immediately revved their engines. It was like a war cry.

Standing in the middle of them were Phil and Mike. There was no sign of Neil. Josh edged forward. Alex followed him. They were standing on one of Pat's 'gardens'. The noise from the mopeds suddenly stopped. There was silence except for a couple of bikes backfiring, until someone screeched out Josh's name from the back of the school.

Neil hurtled into view, half-standing on a red

moped. 'Who's he nicked that from?' whispered Alex to Josh.

Neil called out Josh's name again but he remained quite a distance away from him. It was like a gunfight from an ancient western. Only this time Josh was completely unarmed, while Neil . . .

Neil revved the engine loudly, threateningly. It sounded like a massive dog growling, a dog straining to be let off the leash.

The moped was pointed right at Josh. The noise was deafening. It filled Josh's head. He couldn't see Neil any more. He was hidden behind clouds of blue smoke.

Suddenly, Neil's supporters let out a great cheer.

Then Neil came charging forward.

'He's totally lost it,' cried Alex, sprinting off.

From the safety of the reception Alex yelled at Josh to run.

The boys were yelling too as the bike came screeching towards Josh. He didn't move. Not because he was brave but because at last he knew what this was all about. Josh dug his hands into his trusty Crombie coat pockets. His feet felt strangely light, as if he weren't quite touching the ground. Otherwise he felt surprisingly calm. The bike came hurtling nearer and nearer to him. Any second now, Josh and the bike would collide and Josh would go flying into the air.

But it wasn't Josh who went soaring into the air – it was Neil. At the very last moment he tried to put on the brakes. He'd left it too late. He swerved violently and pitched forward right over the handlebars. He came crashing on to the grass with a small, undignified thud. His bike fell beside him, its wheels spinning wildly.

Neil lay there, struggling to get up again, like a boxer who's been knocked down but is desperate to get back on his feet before he's declared out. Only Neil tried to get up too quickly and lost his balance, toppling over on to the muddy grass again.

Alex, who was standing beside Josh now, started to laugh. At first there were just a few ragged laughs from Josh's supporters, then came this great roar of savage laughter.

Josh didn't laugh.

He was too shocked, not by the fact that Neil was rolling about uncertainly in the mud, but because a terrible, bright red colour had invaded Neil's whole face. He had allowed himself to show embarrassment. It was as if he'd waved a flag of surrender.

Alex saw it too and taunted, 'Beamer, beamer.' Then he explained, 'I didn't run away, Josh. I just thought that guy's such a nutter there's no telling what he'd do.'

'I was pretty certain he wouldn't do anything,' said Josh quietly.

'How did you work that out?' demanded Alex.

Josh shrugged. He wasn't sure what had finally tipped him off. Perhaps it was seeing Mike amongst Neil's cronies. When Mike warned Josh two days ago, he was still acting on Neil's orders. Neil wanted to get Josh worried and, of course, threats were Neil's currency. Threats and stupid stunts and gestures: like riding a moped at someone.

But Neil never did anything. He wasn't even much of a fighter. Come to think of it, Josh couldn't remember Neil ever being in a fight. He was just a master illusionist, picking his victims with great care and convincing everyone he was the power-broker at the centre of a great web of intrigue. He'd fooled everyone, until tonight, when Josh had suddenly called his bluff.

Neil finally struggled to his feet and then tried to pick up his bike, his face still flaming red. Blood from a cut oozed down his face too.

Pat had joined them now and Alex was telling him what had happened. Pat tapped Josh on the shoulder. 'Well done, lad,' he said. Then he clapped his hands at the boys who were still watching this extraordinary scene. 'Go on, be off with you.'

They left as quietly as shadows. 'And you, clear off too,' said Pat to Neil. 'I've told the police about you.'

Neil didn't answer, didn't look at anyone. There was a leaf in his hair and a big wet patch on his jeans. Alex saw it and nudged Josh. Now everything about Neil was funny.

Neil got on to his bike, his hands still trembling. He tried to rev the engine, but it obstinately refused to come to life. In the end, Neil had to get off the bike again and push it away.

Pat called out, 'And don't come back here again.'

'Just give us a wave when you're on *Crimewatch*,' called Alex. He rubbed his hands gleefully. 'He won't dare show his face round here again.'

Josh silently agreed. Neil had let his mask slip, so what other role could he play? He wasn't good at sports. He wasn't clever, cool or good-looking. He didn't wear trendy clothes or have girls flocking round. He didn't have any of the usual things going for him.

By all accounts, he should have been one of the weedy kids. If he returned, that would be the only part left for him.

Neil hadn't just been defeated: he was like a fox after it's been thrown to the hounds. He was in bits.

A great shudder ran through Josh. He didn't want to see any creature in bits, not even Neil.

Josh felt strange, sort of hollow inside – and a bit sick. But this was crazy. Neil didn't deserve pity. When had he ever shown an ounce of pity for his victims? Besides, Neil had brought the whole thing on himself. Josh had been left no choice. It was like amputating an arm because it had gone gangrenous. It certainly wasn't a pleasant thing to do. But it had to be done to stop the disease spreading any further.

Josh had just performed a kind of operation too: purging the school of a deadly virus. Now all the pupils living in fear of Neil were free at last. And a terrible wrong had been righted. He kept telling himself that. But in his head it was still dark.

Alex patted Josh on the back. 'Don't look so serious. We've won. Total victory. Look at him.'

Watching Neil crawl away reminded Josh of that scene in *The Wizard of Oz* where water is poured on the Wicked Witch of the West and she suddenly starts shrinking.

Neil had shrunk nearly as fast as that witch.

He was still shrinking.

Then he vanished completely.

Twelve

Ally knew she wasn't supposed to do this. Only complete amateurs peeked at the audience, though surely it didn't count before a performance had started. She pulled the curtains open just a crack, the way a nosy neighbour might, and stared out. The hall was practically full already and more people were still streaming in. Her gaze lingered on the front row. Only one vacant seat there. Josh wasn't coming.

She couldn't really blame him. Not after the way she'd spoken to him that night. It's just he had no right to plant stolen stamps on anyone, not even Neil. It was a terrible thing to do. And then Josh had tried to place all the blame on her. She was furious. Yet, in a way, he was right. She'd jumped to a wrong conclusion.

That's why she had to go round to Neil's house and apologise. She'd have felt so grubby and horrible inside if she hadn't. She was apologising for her sake, not Neil's. She had stood on Neil's step gabbling to him about the writing on the door and how she'd thought he'd done it and how sorry she was. The light in his hall was dim and she'd only got a blurred impression of him. But his skin seemed a deathly yellow, even his lips looked yellow.

After she'd finished, he spoke in this really drowsy voice, as if he'd just come round from an anaesthetic. 'I wouldn't do anything to hurt you or your mum.' He kept repeating that. And she kept saying, 'I know you wouldn't.' Until finally he said, 'It was nice of you to call,' as if she'd just popped round for a quick chat. Then he closed the door behind him.

That was the last she ever saw of him.

Later in the week Neil's mum had come round to their house when Ally was out. She'd admired the photographs of the new baby, then announced that she and Neil were going away for a while to stay with her sister in Devon. She hinted that she was doing this for Neil's sake.

So now Neil was gone. He needn't stand between her and Josh any more. That had given her the spur to ring Josh two nights ago. It was a terrible, dead conversation. He told her how Neil had come back to the school last week, threatening to drive his moped at Josh. Neil had lost his bottle, just as Josh knew he would. He went on and on about this, as if life was just a competition to see who had the most bottle. Then the conversation suddenly switched to Greg. 'I really have helped him, you know.' He sounded oddly defensive. He didn't ask her once about the play.

The lights were starting to dim. She took one last look. Josh wasn't coming.

Yet, she can see him. He's running towards her. He's giving her his card, saying, 'In case you ever want any help learning your lines.' He's smiling that wonderful, bewitching smile of his.

Now the audience was in darkness. But she can still see him. It's like an arrow through her heart. She stumbled back to the other actors. She couldn't do this without him. The actress playing her mother gave her hand a squeeze. If Ally messed up tonight, the play would be ruined for everyone. And she had worked so hard for this moment.

The curtain began to rise. The stage was alight,

alive. It seemed to be pulling her forward . . .

Greg strolled down the road to school, a new Sherlock Holmes book in his bag. He didn't walk along reading any more. He'd grown out of that. Josh said Greg had grown up a lot over the past few weeks. Greg stored away all the things Josh said to him.

A couple of boys nodded at him. Older boys too. For the past weeks people had been coming up congratulating him for being the one whose plan had rid them of Neil. How they'd all found out was a mystery. Still, Greg didn't mind. Helping to rid the school of Neil was something to be proud of.

Greg slowed down. Phil was across the road. And he was sure Phil had just smiled at him, that ugly, mocking, smirk of his. He'd never liked Phil. In many ways Phil was as bad as Neil. The school would certainly be better off without Phil, too.

They should have another Council of War. Of course, they would have to come up with a completely different plan.

But it could be done. And it would improve the quality of everyone's life.

Greg reached the school gates. Josh would already be in H.Q. He was at school before most of the teachers these days. Greg could slip in and see Josh now, tell him about his proposal for a new Council of War.

He ran excitedly into school.